To my nephews and niece.
Lynn Papa loves you always.

THE WARRIORS OF RAW

Lynn Mathai

AUSTIN MACAULEY PUBLISHERS™

LONDON • CAMBRIDGE • NEW YORK • SHARJAH

Ordering Information:
Quantity sales: special discounts are available on quantity purchases by corporations, associations, and others. For details, contact the publisher at the address below.

Publisher's Cataloging-in-Publication data
Mathai, Lynn
The Warriors of Raw

ISBN 9781643781822 (Paperback)
ISBN 9781643781839 (Hardback)
ISBN 9781645367123 (ePub e-book)

The main category of the book — YOUNG ADULT FICTION / Science Fiction / General

Library of Congress Control Number: 2019912399

www.austinmacauley.com/us

First Published (2019)
Austin Macauley Publishers LLC
40 Wall Street, 28th Floor
New York, NY 10005
USA

mail-usa@austinmacauley.com
+1 (646) 5125767

Thank you Luca Cognata, Jenna Zacharia, Mr. Becker, and Amanda Rios for all your help with this book.

Prologue

Chacko Mathais and his fellow warrior monks, along with their new Wiccan companion Aley, slowly made their way through a dark and narrow passageway. Minutes later, they entered a massive cavern. The rock formation in the cave was so strange that it looked otherworldly. They started to look for a place to hide the bundle that they were commissioned to hide. As they searched, they heard demonic snarling and grunting noises from the outer passageway along with the sound of claws scratching on the walls of the cave. Moments later, Mathais saw a spot in the corner of the cavern which was illuminated by a sliver of light from above.

He called out to the others and pointed to the spot; they all went to the spot and started digging. As they dug deeper and deeper, the grunting and snarling became louder and louder. Mathais began to get worried for their safety; Aley noticed the concern on his face.

"Are you all right?" Aley asked.

"I guess I am okay. I am just worried as to why those demons are not attacking us," Mathais answered.

"Well, there is a simple reason for that. I have placed an enchantment on the cavern so the demons cannot enter," she answered.

"How long will it last?" he asked.

"It should last for all eternity, but that is not a guarantee," she replied.

"What will happen once we leave the cavern?" Mathais asked.

She answered him with a grave look on her face.

"Keep on digging!" he called out.

When they had dug deep enough, Mathais placed the bundle into the hole and covered it up with dirt. Aley then placed a concealment spell on the hiding place and a final protection spell on the cavern. They all shook each other's hands like they were never going to see each other again and left the cavern with weapons in hand. As they entered the passageway, the flames of their torches blew out and they were engulfed in darkness as they prepared for the battle of their lives.

Chapter 1

A New Heir in the Line of Succession

There was a great evil in the land of Old York New that popped up from time to time. This great evil had many names, but it was most commonly referred to as the Black Shadows. The Black Shadows have existed since the dawn of time and only one group of young warriors could stop this evil; the Warriors of Raw. This is their beginning.

Old York New was a peacefully quiet land with many territories, where justice and harmony ran true from the previous ruler to the next. The towns and farms were spacious; the bodies of water and rolling valleys looked majestic. Most of the people in the land were civil to their neighbors. Lord Devon had recently been crowned king and sat on the throne. He gathered all his councilmen together in the council room.

"Lord Devon, we have spoken amongst ourselves and we think you should appoint a royal heir in the line of succession for yourself," one of the councilpersons said.

"But why should I need one when I have a loyal and faithful council like you along with a wonderful wife that helps me?" Lord Devon asked.

"We councilmen are old fossils; something could happen to us at any time. And if God forbid the queen falls ill, what shall you do?" another councilman asked.

"I do not know why you would say such a thing. But if it is this important to you, then I shall appoint a royal heir in the line of succession," Lord Devon answered. "Gather the gentlemen in the kingdom so I can see who may be well suited for the position."

That afternoon, the royal councilmen gathered all the honorable and loyal men of Old York New. From noblemen to farmers, there was a long line that stretched out to the castle's main gates. The assessments lasted all afternoon and well into the evening. Not finding anyone suitable yet, Lord Devon gave the remaining men lodging for the night and retired himself.

In the morning, everybody in the castle enjoyed a breakfast feast, after which the assessments continued. As the morning turned into afternoon, Lord Devon conversed with all the men to contemplate how promising they were. As the long day drew on, Lord Devon began to feel tired and got ready to return to his quarters.

The night sky was filled with stars that looked like diamonds, and as he was leaving the veranda, a young man with dark brown hair, dressed in the clothing of a nobleman, addressed Lord Devon introducing himself as Keals. They both spoke for an hour, before Lord Devon went to his quarters and retired. The following morning after breakfast, Lord Devon gathered all his councilmen with Queen Bella at Lord Devon's right-hand side for support.

"I have chosen an heir in the line of succession. The young gentleman named Keals of Niyon shall be my heir in the line of succession."

"Yes, but can you and this Kingdom put our faith in such a person?" Queen Bella asked.

"I had a talk with him and I believe he is trustworthy. I really think we can place our trust in him," replied Lord Devon. "Gather all the people in the kingdom and inform them that I will be holding a coronation ceremony for Keals of Niyon."

Moments later, they left the council room and started the preparations for the coronation ceremony.

Meanwhile, on the outskirts of the main village, stood a little farm. A young man and woman were doing farm chores while three children were playing around. The children were playing in a tree, seeing who could climb the highest. The first boy had short black hair and black eyes. The girl had long black hair and beautiful dark brown eyes. The second boy had black hair that puffed up a little and he had black eyes. The two boys were athletic and toned while the girl was slim and the three of them appeared to be about the same age. The three children were of Indian background.

All of a sudden, the children saw a royal messenger on horseback approaching in the distance. The two boys climbed slightly higher into the tree and hoisted the girl onto the branch that they were on. They sat there watching in silence as the horse stopped in front of them. The messenger said something and handed the adults a rolled up piece of parchment, then the messenger got back on his horse and rode away. The young woman and man started to talk.

All of a sudden, they both went into the farmhouse cabin and a minute later the woman came back out. She came looking for the children making her way over to the tree. She couldn't find them so she got scared.

"We are up here," the taller boy called out.

"You children nearly gave me heart failure. Now come down from there before you get hurt," the young lady told the kids.

"Okay mother, we are sorry," the taller boy answered.

The children jumped down from the tree and the four of them went back to the cabin.

"Kids, we have been invited to the castle to attend the coronation ceremony of the new heir in the line of succession," the woman told the children.

"Are our parents attending also?" the shorter boy and the girl asked.

"Of course they will be attending. Everybody in the kingdom will be there," the young man replied.

They heard a horse and wagon approaching so they went outside. A woman and man stopped in front of the cabin and jumped down from the wagon.

"Hello mother, hello father. We have missed you," the girl and shorter boy said at the same time.

"We have missed you as well Brandon and Madison. Well if it is not Liza, Boby, and Isaiah," the woman said.

"Joseph, Anna, how was your journey here?" Liza asked.

"Our journey was well," Joseph replied. "Ruth has sent word that she will meet us at the coronation ceremony."

The children continued playing as the parents helped Liza and Boby finish the farm chores. Meanwhile at the castle, preparations were being made for the coronation ceremony. Keals of Niyon was resting in quarters two doors away from Devon and Bella's. All of a sudden there was a knock at the door. Keals slowly got up from the bed and opened the door. A chamber maiden greeted him and let him know that Lord Devon wanted to see him. After the chamber maiden left, Keals got ready.

Two armed guards stood at the doors of the throne room. The guards greeted Keals with a salute and led him into the throne room where Lord Devon and Queen Bella were sitting on their thrones holding hands.

"Are you ready for the ceremony?" Lord Devon asked.

"Not really, but I will be," Keals replied.

"Do not fear, I felt the same way the day of my coronation as King. But I did fine," explained Lord Devon. "And you will do fine as well."

Around noon time the castle chapel began filling up with people from around the kingdom. In half an hour, the chapel was packed; the remaining people lined the back walls. Beautiful music filled the air. A line of monks slowly walked down the aisle, followed by Lord Devon, Queen Bella, and Keals of Niyon.

The music trickled down to a whisper and the monks started singing hymns. Once the monks stopped singing, everyone rose from their seats. The head monk stood in front of the congregation. Lord Devon took his sword and pressed it against both of Keals' shoulders.

"Will you promise to govern the people of Old York New and of your possessions and territories to any belonging or pertaining, according to their true laws and customs?" the head monk asked.

"I promise to do so," Keals answered.

"Will you cause law and justice, in mercy, to be executed in all your judgment?" the monk farther asked.

"I promise to do so," Keals answered.

"Will you maintain the laws of God with true profession? Will you maintain the inviolable settlement of the church of Old York New established in Old York New?" the monk finally said.

"All this I promise to do. The things which I have here before promised, I will perform and keep. So help me God," Keals answered.

"Then by the powers that are invested in me from God, I dub thee heir in the line of succession."

The monk made the sign of the cross on Keals; Keals turned around. The chapel erupted in applause with clapping and whistling. The crowd lined up to congratulate Keals, and later they were invited to an evening banquet.

Chapter 2
The Black Shadows

As days passed after the coronation, a storm was brewing. Meanwhile on the farm on the outskirts of the village, the children were playing; Boby and Liza were doing farm chores. All of a sudden, the sky whirled pitch black. The sky was lit by lightning and claps of thunder. Just then lightning struck a tree the children were playing near, splitting it and setting it ablaze. Brandon and Isaiah grabbed pails, filled them with water, and began throwing water at the blazing tree. Madison ran to get Liza and Boby, and they helped put out the fire. The sky became even darker, so they put the animals back into their pens and went back inside.

The rain started to pour and the castle was quiet to a whisper. All around the castle, candles were lit giving off the only gentle light. Lord Devon and Queen Bella were in the throne room talking and holding hands. The sweet aromas of lunch being made filled the air.

Keals was in his quarters writing a letter, when suddenly out of the only light in the room appeared a dark black shadow, in the form of a large man. Slowly, another shadow appeared and then another. Suddenly the shadows started whispering strange things to Keals. Keals covered his ears with his hands to silence the whispering but could not block it. All around the castle the Black Shadows appeared, whispering.

As fast as they came, the Black Shadows had left the castle. Immediately after Keals saw and heard the shadows, he went to the throne room. Lord Devon and Queen Bella were talking with the councilmen. Keals knocked on the door and went inside.

"I am sorry to intrude but I must talk to you my lord," Keals said.

"There is no need to apologize, come in," Lord Devon replied.

"I have seen strange shadows in my quarters whispering strange things," Keals said.

"I know about these Black Shadows. Messages from all over the kingdom have arrived with similar complaints," Lord Devon replied.

Moments later, a royal messenger knocked on the doors and entered the room; he handed a councilman a folded-up piece of parchment and left the room again. The councilman unfolded the piece of parchment and read it.

"There have been reports of the same happenings in the south of our kingdom," the councilman said.

"Go with a group of my knights to the south and see if you can help the people," Lord Devon said to the head councilman. Then he turned to Keals. "You accompany them as well on this journey."

First thing at daybreak, they were packed and ready for the journey. After breakfast, they got on their horses and left. Half an hour later they finally made their way out of the main village and took to a side road. Soon it began getting dark; they found a quiet place to set up camp so they settled in for the night.

They got an early start at daybreak and made good time; by late afternoon they reached the south lands. People came up to them begging for help. Keals saw the sadness and grief in the people's face. Was all this sadness and grief due to the Black Shadows' arrival? The councilmen, Keals, and the knights got off their horses and went to speak with the people. The people explained that the Black Shadows whispered to them to do terrible things. While most of them resisted the Black Shadows' temptations, others could not. The latter had ravaged and destroyed town properties.

As the knights started to help rebuild the destroyed parts of the towns, Keals and the councilmen helped pay for food and other necessities. They all worked day and night tirelessly to restore balance and order to the area. Days slowly passed and soon their work was done. The group got their things together, got their horses ready for the journey and left the south lands.

Chapter 3
New Unlikely Friends

Making good time, they arrived back to the castle sooner than they expected. They reported their findings to Lord Devon and Queen Bella, who were deeply troubled.

Meanwhile back at the farm Madison, Isaiah, and Brandon were playing in the field near the farm. Slowly making their way closer and closer to the forest's edge, when suddenly the three of them were startled by movements all around them. Brandon and Isaiah kept looking for anything unusual but found nothing. Just then a small ball of fur leaped into Madison's arms, it was a cheetah cub. The cheetah cub jumped out of Madison's arms again and into the foliage again.

The kids went to work quickly to look for the cub. The cheetah cub was hiding in the hollowed out roots of a very old tree. Madison scooped the little cub up into her arms and started petting it.

"He must be lost," Madison said.

"How do you know it is a male?" Isaiah asked.

"It is very clear. Look," Madison answered as she picked it up and showed them its undersides.

"Where do you think he came from," Brandon asked.

"I do not know. Maybe Ruth would know," Madison answered, "I will ask her when she comes."

Madison held the cub up on her shoulders, and they left. When they got back to the farm, Madison put the cheetah cub onto one of the beds and they began playing with the cub. Isaiah went back outside to look for his parents but didn't see them so he went inside again. Sometime later the cub started purring sadly. Madison went over to the fire pit, made a fire, and warmed up some milk. She poured the warm milk into a bottle and gave it to the cub, who began to suck on the bottle happily with excitement. When he finished drinking, he licked his mouth clean and licked Madison and the boys with thanks.

As they continued to play with the cub, a gust of wind blew through the window, and suddenly there was a knock at the door. Isaiah went and opened the door only to find Ruth, the family friend. She was wearing a long white gown with a white cloak; her wild hair was so long it reached her hips.

"I sensed you needed me so I came right over," Ruth said.

"That was fast," Brandon commented.

"Like I have explained to you children before; the sorcery I use heightens all my senses," Ruth said as she held Brandon's hand.

"We found him in the forest," Madison said as she picked up the cub. "And we wondered if you had any idea where he might have come from."

"Well, he might have come from the traveling carnival that was in town a few days ago," Ruth replied.

"It is truly sad that they left him all alone to fend for himself like that," Isaiah said as he petted the cub.

"They might not even know that they left him behind," Ruth said.

"Do you think my parents would let me keep him?" Isaiah asked.

"I do not know if that is a safe idea, but if nobody claims him, I will talk to your parents about it," Ruth replied with a smile. "Would you like to come and see little Scottie?"

"We would like that," Madison replied. "Why did he not come with you anyway?"

"He has not been feeling well for the past couple of days," Ruth replied.

"Are the horses in the stables and the wagon in the back?" Ruth asked.

"I am pretty sure that they are there," Isaiah answered. "But why can you not just teleport us to your cottage?"

"Because the sorcery I yield is not that powerful. Besides, teleporting all of us would use up all my strength," Ruth explained. "Oh, bring the cub, he might cheer up Scottie."

Isaiah wrote a note on a piece of parchment and left it on the dining table. They left the cabin and Isaiah locked the door behind him. When they got to the stables Ruth hitched the wagon to two horses, then they got on and rode away. When they got to Ruth's cottage, Isaiah tied the horses up and they went inside.

"Mother, is that you?" a boy's soft, sickly voice called out.

"Yes, my dear," Ruth answered, "and I have a surprise for you."

Madison, Brandon, and Isaiah walked into a small room and found little Scottie lying on a bed. Scottie had brown hair and eyes; when he stood up, he was only as tall as Isaiah's shoulders. He tried to get up when suddenly Scottie felt weak so he sat on the bed.

"Ruth told us that you were feeling better. But it does not look like that is true to me," Madison said.

"My mother is right. I am much better," Scottie said.

"Well, we have something that will cheer you up even more," Madison said.

She picked up the cub and placed him on the bed. Scottie smiled at them and started petting the cub.

"Where did you get him?"

"We found him in the forest near Isaiah's farm," Brandon answered.

They continued to play with the cheetah cub as the afternoon sky slowly got darker and turned into evening. Ruth made a fire in the fire pit and placed a pot filled with water on the fire. All of a sudden, they heard horses approaching and moments later there was a knock at the door. Ruth opened the door, it was Isaiah's parents.

"Hi Liza, Boby. How are you?" Ruth asked.

"We are good. We have come to get the children," Liza replied smiling. "How is little Scottie feeling?"

"I am doing much better," Scottie said as he came out of the room and hugged Liza. "Thanks for asking."

Just then Madison, Isaiah, and Brandon came out of the room as well.

"Children, are you ready to go?" Liza asked.

"You are not going anywhere until you have some supper," Ruth said.

They all washed up at the well in the back of the cottage. The kids set the table, and then everyone sat down, said grace, and started eating. For dinner, they had mutton stew and mugs of ale. Isaiah and Ruth told Liza and Boby about the cheetah cub, and they argued over wanting to keep him. After dinner, Isaiah took the cub as they all went outside. Liza untied the horses and hitched the wagon to them. They got on the wagon and rode away as Ruth and Scottie waved farewell. On the way, they dropped Madison and Brandon home.

The following morning, Isaiah woke up and yawned. He looked around the room, but the cub was nowhere to be found. Suddenly, he heard soft purring coming from underneath his bed. Isaiah got out of his bed and knelt on the floor; the cub was curled up in a ball by the wall. He gave the cub some milk and started his morning chores.

Meanwhile, back at the castle, everything was calm and quiet. Lord Devon and his councilmen were in the council room talking when Keals walked into the room.

"I am sorry to interrupt you, but I received word that the Black Shadows has been to the west land of Old York New," Keals said.

"Send help and provisions to the west land," Devon said.

"I have already dispatched help and provisions to that region," Keals said.

"I am pleased that you are on top of all this," Lord Devon said. "What are you doing at this present moment?"

"I am going back to my quarters; I have to finish signing those declarations you wanted me to sign."

"Okay, but not before you have lunch with the queen and I," Devon said as they entered the dining hall.

The following morning at the farm, Brandon and Madison came and helped Isaiah with his morning chores. As they worked, they talked.

"What did your mother and father say about the cub? Are they allowing you to keep him?" Madison asked.

"I am not sure," Isaiah answered.

Just then his parents called him from the doorway, so he went inside and sat down.

"We know why Brandon and Madison came early this morning. They want to know about the cub," Liza said as she petted and played with the cub. "Your father and I have discussed it and we decided that if nobody claims him by the next full moon, you may keep him."

"And this will also be a good lesson in responsibility," Boby said.

"He also fell in love with the cub," Liza whispered to Isaiah as they both rolled their eyes and laughed.

Isaiah went back outside and did thumbs up at Madison and Brandon. They both smiled and continued to work. A little while later, they saw Ruth and little Scottie in the distance approaching the farm. Moments later they arrived, Scottie had a ball in his hands.

"Hi Ruth, hi little Scottie. How are you doing? What are you doing here?" Isaiah asked.

"We need to go into town to pick up our provisions. So, we came to ask your parents if we can use your wagon," Ruth said.

She went inside the cabin while Scottie sat with them.

"How are you feeling?" Isaiah asked Scottie.

"I feel much better. I just have a tiny cough now," he replied.

"Guess what? My parents said that if nobody claims the cub then I could keep him," Isaiah told Scottie.

"That is really good," Little Scottie said. "What are you going to name him?"

"I do not think we should name him just yet. What if we get too attached to him and then we end up having to give him up?" Isaiah answered.

"I do not think you have to worry about that. If someone was going to claim him, they would have come by now," Scottie said.

Just then Ruth walked out of the cabin.

"Liza said you may come with us into town," Ruth said.

"But will our parents not worry about us?" Brandon asked.

"Liza is sending word to them right now," Ruth said.

She hitched the wagon to the horses; they climbed on and rode away. When they got to town, Ruth tied the horses up and they walked around town. The kids were kicking around Scottie's ball when all of a sudden Scottie bumped into someone. He looked up to see who it was and apologize, it was a castle guard.

"I am so sorry. Please forgive me," Scottie said.

The guard frowned at Scottie and slapped him across the face.

"How dare you touch me, peasant," the guard said to Scottie.

Ruth saw what happened and stepped in front of the guard.

"He apologized to you, why did you do that to my son?" Ruth asked angrily "I think you better apologize. You do not want anything bad to happen to you."

"Who do you think you are talking to?" the guard snarled. "Is that a threat?"

"I think I need to teach a fool some manners," Ruth said.

Ruth began chanting and all of a sudden the guard slowly floated off the ground and was carried higher and higher into the air. A crowd of people formed around Ruth and the children, but seconds later the crowd separated and a group of guards with Lord Devon appeared.

"What is the meaning of all of this?" Lord Devon asked.

"Nothing, I am just teaching this pig some manners," Ruth answered as she turned to see who was talking.

When she saw it was Lord Devon, she stopped chanting and the guard fell hard onto the ground. The guard slowly stood up and limped over to the other guards. Lord Devon asked what had happened and Ruth explained everything. Devon stared at the guard with disappointment.

"Is this true?" Lord Devon asked the guard.

"Yes, it is."

"Then apologize to them right now," Devon ordered him.

"I am sorry for what happened," the guard said through gritted teeth to Scottie and Ruth.

"I will personally reprimand him later, but for now as my sincerest apologies I will personally give you a guided visit of the castle," Lord Devon said.

"Thank you. But we must not," Ruth said.

"Yes, but I insist," Lord Devon said. "And I will not take 'No' for an answer."

When they all got to the castle, Lord Devon showed them around. Ruth and the kids walked around taking in all the sights and sounds. They slowly made their way to the throne room, and Devon personally introduced the group to Queen Bella. A little later, Devon and a small group of guards escorted the children and Ruth back to town to purchase provisions.

Chapter 4

Whispers and Betrayals

The heat of the summer began to die down, and the calm breeze of fall drifted through the air. Days passed by slowly and two full moons had come and gone yet nobody had claimed the cub. Remembering their promise, his parents let Isaiah keep the cub. Two weeks after the second full moon passed, Madison and Brandon came for a visit. The children went outside with the cub and began playing with him and talking.

"What are you going to name him?" Brandon asked.

"Well, he is a very tricky little guy," Isaiah said happily. "What do you think of the name Fabian?"

"I do not know if that would be a good name for him. He does not look like a Fabian," Madison said with a strange look. "What about the name Cheats, I like that name for him."

"He looks like a Cheats," Brandon added.

"I like that name. From now on he shall be called Cheats," Isaiah said.

Then they continued to play with Cheats the cub. The rest of the day was uneventful as the kids helped with the farm chores.

Back at the castle, Queen Bella was making preparations for a journey to another kingdom for a royal summit as Keals came into the throne room.

"I am sorry to bother you but have you seen Lord Devon?" Keals asked.

"No, but I would like to talk to you, if you have the time," Queen Bella replied.

"I always have time for you," Keals said.

"While I am gone would you look after Devon for me?" Bella asked.

"Of course, I will," Keals answered.

"Thank you," Queen Bella said as she smiled at Keals.

Just then the doors of the throne room creaked open and one of the royal messengers walked in.

"The carriage is ready for your journey your highness," the messenger said.

"Thank you very much," Bella replied to the messenger. Then she turned to Keals once again, "Just remember the promise you made to me."

"Do not worry your highness," Keals assured.

The three of them left the throne room, and Bella made her way to her and Devon's quarters. The messenger entered the quarters, grabbed Bella's bags, and left again. All of a sudden Devon entered the room and kissed Bella. Then they held each other's hands as they left the quarters, making their way to the main gates of the castle. Keals was standing and waiting for them near the carriage. Bella embraced Devon again and slowly climbed into the carriage. The carriage pulled off and Bella waved farewell to Lord Devon and Keals with a sad look on her face. She stared at both of them until they were out of sight.

Keals and Lord Devon slowly made their way back into the castle as they both talked. Meanwhile in town, Ruth and Scottie were walking around when they noticed something strange happening. There was a group of people that were acting strange and looked even stranger. Their eyes were all very dark, almost pitch black; their skin was extremely pale and flaky, and they were speaking in a language that Ruth and Scottie did not recognize. The group started to leave so the pair followed them.

They followed the group through town and ended up in a narrow passageway. Ruth and Scottie hid behind a pile of sacks. All of a sudden, the whole group of people shook violently and screamed, writhing in agony. They fell to the ground, lying there totally still. Suddenly translucent forms oozed out of the people, turning into the Black Shadows with glowing eyes. Ruth and Scottie gasped in fear and shock.

"We better get out of here before something bad happens to us," Ruth said.

"For once in my life, I fully agree with you," Scottie whispered back to her.

They both ran out of the passageway as if their lives depended on it. They ran to the castle to warn Lord Devon of what they've seen, only to be turned away by the guards. So they both left town. When they were just outside town, Ruth teleported them the rest of the way.

Seconds later they both appeared with a loud pop in front of Isaiah's parents' cabin. Ruth knocked on the door but nobody answered, so she banged on the door. Just then the door creaked open and Isaiah peaked out of the opening. He opened the door wider and they quickly walked in, and Isaiah closed the door behind them. Liza and Boby were sitting at the table drinking tea; Ruth sat down and told them about the events they had seen.

"We must inform Lord Devon of these events," Liza said.

"I went to the castle and tried to let him know but the guards did not let me," Ruth said.

"Then we will just have to send a message with a hawk," Liza said.

Ruth wrote a note on a piece of parchment and rolled it up, and she and Liza went outside. Liza took their messenger hawk out of a large cage. Ruth tied the parchment to the hawk's claw as Liza whispered to it, then the hawk flew away. About a half-hour later the hawk flew through the opened window and perched itself on Liza's shoulders. A little while later Ruth and Scottie bid them farewell and teleported back to their cottage. The sky slowly got darker and darker until it became as black as satin cloth and the stars twinkled high above.

The following morning, after Ruth and little Scottie finished breakfast they sat around and talked. Just then, they heard a knock at the door. Scottie went and opened the door, it was a royal messenger. He presented himself and they let him inside. He let them know that their presents were requested by Lord Devon to discuss the events they saw the other day.

"May I bring my son as well?" Ruth asked.

"Of course you may," the messenger replied.

They left the cottage and Ruth locked the door behind herself. They climbed into the royal carriage and rode away. When they got to the castle, they climbed out of the carriage, the messenger led them to the throne room. Minutes later Lord Devon, Keals, and the council members came into the room.

"I am sorry we kept you waiting. We had matters to take care of," Devon said.

"No apology is necessary," Ruth said.

"Now, tell us what you witnessed the other day," Devon said.

Then Ruth and Scottie explained to them what they saw.

"And these events happened exactly as you are telling us?" Devon asked.

"Yes, it happened exactly this way," Ruth answered.

"This is new information. We did not know these Black Shadows could take possession of people," Keals said.

"We have to do a sweep of all of Old York New to search for any others that have been possessed," one of the council members said.

"That would be mad. We cannot do a sweep of Old York New," Devon argued.

"If I may be so bold, I know this spell that can detect evil things," Ruth interrupted softly. "It will work to a distance of twenty kilometers."

"If we make this journey, can you come along to assist us?" Devon asked Ruth.

"Of course, I can Lord Devon."

"You may go for now. We will send word to you when we are ready," Devon said.

Just then Devon called for a messenger, Devon told the messenger to take Ruth and Scottie back home. Then they left the throne room and the messenger led them to the main gates. The three of them climbed into the carriage and it pulled off. Half an hour later they got to the cottage, Ruth and Scottie bid the messenger farewell and went inside and they began their chores.

The next morning at the farm, Isaiah woke up early and began playing with Cheats the cub. A little while later he warmed up some milk and fed Cheats. After, Cheats licked his mouth clean and licked Isaiah's face in thanks. Throughout the day they heard strange whispering. They kept ever vigilant, keeping in mind the events that Ruth and Scottie had witnessed.

As evening drew near, Liza and Isaiah saw someone approaching from the distance. As the person got closer, they realized it was Boby. He was waddling from side to side as he was walking unsteadily. He was singing to himself and his voice was slurred. He was in a drunken state. Isaiah and Liza ran over to him and helped him into the cabin, they laid him on a bed and left. A while later Liza went to where Boby was lying down.

"Get up, supper is ready," Liza said.

"Okay, I am coming," Boby answered.

"I know that you have been paying the town wench for her time and company. Is that where you got the rash and the itching? Is that why you need the ointment? Did you think I would not find out?"

Boby looked at Liza with surprise that she had known.

"Now, get up," Liza said to Boby again. "You cannot keep coming home in this condition, it is not good for Isaiah."

At that moment Isaiah came to the doorway.

"Do not worry about me. I have gotten used to father being in this condition," Isaiah said.

That evening the three of them ate in silence and went to bed.

The following morning at Ruth's cottage everything was quiet. Ruth was preparing breakfast when they heard screeching from outside, all of a sudden a hawk swooped in through the window and landed on the table. Ruth untied a piece of parchment, unrolled it, and read it. She told Scottie what the note said and then told Scottie to pack up a sack with clothes. Minutes later they grabbed their bags and left. Ruth checked to see if anyone was watching. After she cleared the coast, she held Scottie's hand and they teleported away.

They popped up near a cottage; this cottage was smaller than their own. The door of the cottage was set to the right of the front of the house. There were only two windows in the cottage. The first was in the front just to the left of the door, the second was on the right side of the cottage. They both went to the door and Ruth knocked on it. Seconds later Brandon opened it, they went inside and Brandon closed the door.

"You have not been over for a while," Joseph said as Ruth hugged them. "How are you doing?"

"We are just fine. May little Scottie stay here for a few days?" Ruth asked.

"Of course, he may stay," Anna replied worryingly. "But are you sure everything is okay?"

"Everything is fine, Lord Devon wants me to help him with a journey and it will take a few days," Ruth replied.

"Well, Scottie is definitely welcome to stay," Joseph added.

"Thank you so much, I owe you one," Ruth said to Anna and Joseph. Then she turned to Scottie "I will be back in a few days. And make sure you behave yourself."

"I promise I will," Scottie replied.

Ruth kissed Scottie on the cheek, hugged the others, and left the cottage. She moved away from the cottage and quickly teleported away.

Ruth popped up at the outskirts of town and walked the rest of the way to the castle. The guards saw her coming and slowly opened the gates; they greeted her and led her to the throne room. A few minutes later Lord Devon, Keals, one of the councilmen, and a very small group of guards entered the room.

"This is my head councilman Sir Tier," Devon said to Ruth.

"It is nice to meet you," Ruth said.

"Same to you and the pleasure is all mine," sir Tier replied.

"We will be leaving shortly," Devon said.

Minutes later one of the messengers came in and told them the horses were ready for their journey. They grabbed their bags and the other supplies and left. They got to the horses, climbed on and galloped away. The sounds of crunching leaves and galloping horses filled the air. The wind blew through their hair more and more as they picked up speed. A couple of hours later they reached a distant village in Old York New. They dismounted their horses and Sir Tier announced why they were there. Ruth chanted an incantation and all the villagers froze in place.

Ruth made a small fire and made a protective circle around her and the fire. Then she took out a small pot from her bag and placed it on the flames. She added herbs and other ingredients to the pot and started chanting once again. All of a sudden, two people shook violently and fell to the ground, laying there motionless. Ruth quickly emptied out the pot. Just then the two people's necks began to swallow and bulge and two Black Shadows came out of their mouths. Ruth quickly chanted a binding spell, and both Black Shadows froze in midair. Seconds later they unfroze, squirmed a little, and suddenly they vanished. The small group packed up their stuff, bid farewell to the villagers, and rode out of the village.

Meanwhile back at the castle, Keals was sitting at a table reading over documents in his quarters. The only light in the room came from a candle on the table. Just then a Black Shadow materialized from out of nowhere. It slowly glided out of the shadows and into the light; Keals looked at it in terror.

"I've come in peace. I will not harm you," the Black Shadow hissed.

"I do not believe you. Be gone you evil creature," Keals said.

"We Black Shadows are of the shadows, but we only tell you certain truths," the creature hissed with a smirk. "And I can tell you about the time to come."

"These are all lies. The only thing that you creatures do is destroy," Keals snarled.

"I'm not lying to you, I tell you the truth," the Black Shadow whispered. "Your Lord Devon will bring darkness and destruction to the kingdom of Old York New."

"These are all lies," Keals shouted.

"This is the truth and I can show you," the creature said.

The Black Shadow waved its left hand in the air, and then it held Keals' face with its ice-cold hands and its eyes glowed really brightly. The Black Shadow began showing Keals a false vision:

It was a dark and rainy day. People were lined up in the courtyard of the castle; they were shackled and handcuffed, with dismal expressions on their face. Devon was sitting on a throne, his eyes were pitch-black and he had a malevolent smirk on his face. He was wearing long black leather robes, and he wheeled a whip with sharp spikes at the end. Queens Bella looked evil as well and she was also wearing long black leather robes. A man in handcuff and shackles dropped to his knees and started pleading to Lord Devon. Devon kicked him to the ground and began whipping him with the spiked whip. Devon kicked the man again, and he and Bella chuckled evilly.

Keals stared at this vision with a blank look on his face. As he looked at these events, the Black Shadow whispered into his ears and Keals mumbled to himself. The images faded and the creature took its hands off Keals' head.

"These things will come to pass," the Black Shadow said. "But you can stop these things from happening if you join us."

"Leave me alone you devil," Keals said.

"As you wish," the Black Shadow whispered.

The Black Shadow glided towards the shadows and suddenly disappeared.

It was getting darker and Ruth and the small group of travelers were still on the road. At the present moment, they were slowly galloping on a narrow roadway in the middle of a wooded area. The sounds of crunching leaves and insects buzzing around fill the air. Moments later they slowed down to a halt.

"We should set up camp here for the night," Ruth suggested.

They all unpacked their equipment and set up camp.

"I am going to retire for the night. Goodnight," Ruth said.

"You are not eating supper with us?" Devon asked.

"I am not really hungry," Ruth said.

She went into one of the tents and went to sleep, while the others ate supper and talked.

The following morning the group woke up at dawn, packed up the supplies, and they slowly left. Back at Anna and Joseph's cottage, the kids were playing ball when Isaiah came over with Cheats trailing behind him. Just then Madison, Brandon, and Scottie stopped playing ball and the kids began playing with Cheats. Later that afternoon the kids helped Anna and Joseph with the chores while Cheats chased butterflies around the cottage. After lunch, Anna and Joseph went to town to pick up their provisions while the kids and Cheats stayed behind. Later that day they came back from town and the kids helped them unload the provisions.

After supper, Anna dropped Isaiah and Cheats back to the farm.

A few days had passed since Queen Bella and the small group had been gone. Keals was in his quarters resting on his bed. He hadn't had a good night's sleep ever since the Black Shadow had approached him. He had kept on hearing voices whispering to him. All of a sudden, the same Black Shadow that came the other day appeared. Its eyes began glowing brightly and it stared into Keals' eyes.

"So, will you help us stop Lord Devon?" the Black Shadow asked. "You know I speak the truth."

"I will help you put a stop to Lord Devon," Keals said staring blankly into the glowing eyes.

Chapter 5
The Death of Royalty

A few days had passed and the small group of travelers finally came back from their journey. Keals was waiting for them in the courtyard of the castle. Lord Devon asked Ruth if she wanted to stay for lunch but she declined, so Lord Devon told a messenger to escort Ruth home.

A while later Ruth teleported herself to the cottage were Scottie was staying. She knocked on the door and Joseph opened it. Ruth greeted Anna and Joseph and sat down at the dining table. Just then Scottie, Madison, and Brandon came out of a room; Scottie ran over to Ruth and hugged her.

"I missed you mother," Scottie said.

"I missed you as well my boy," Ruth said to him.

"How was your journey?" Joseph asked.

"It was good and very productive," Ruth answered.

"Did you find a lot of people possessed by the Black Shadows?" Scottie asked.

"We found quite a few. But not as much as we thought we would," Ruth said with a smile. "Did you behave yourself?"

"He was a very good boy," Anna answered.

"Scottie, get your stuff. We must be going," Ruth said.

"You cannot leave just yet. Lunch is ready! I am sure you are hungry," Anna said.

"We have things to do when we get back home," Ruth said.

"I insist that you stay for lunch," Anna said.

When they had finished eating, they all washed up. Ruth and Scottie said farewell and left. As they walked, Ruth and Scottie talked about their days apart from each other. A little while later they reached their cottage, went inside, and began their chores.

Back at Liza and Boby's farm, Boby was lying down from a drunken stupor while Liza and Isaiah were feeding the farm animals. Afterward, they played with Cheats. As the day progressed, it began getting cooler and cooler. Later Cheats purred sadly so Isaiah gave him some warm milk. It slowly got darker so they went inside for supper.

The following day at the castle Lord Devon woke up at sunrise. He got ready for the day and took a short walk in the castle's gardens. All of a sudden, a hawk swooped down and perched itself on Devon's shoulders. Devon untied a parchment from its talons and read it, and then he called for a messenger. When the messenger came, Devon informed her that Queen Bella would be coming in two hours' time and to make preparations for her arrival. The messenger quickly left leaving him alone again. A big smile of cheerfulness swept over Devon's face and he went to the throne room.

The castle's atmosphere was much more cheerful and brighter with the preparations of Queen Bella's arrival. Flower arrangements were being placed at almost every corner of the castle. A red carpet was placed from the main courtyard to the main entranceway. The wonderful aromas of a large feast being made filled the air. In his quarters Keals was pacing back and forth as he thought to himself. Was the Black Shadow telling him the truth about Devon?

Was he really going to help them? Suddenly a messenger knocked on the door and came in, he informed Keals that Lord Devon was calling for him. They both left the room.

As Keals was walking through the corridors, he could hear the Black Shadows whispering to him. Moments later he reached the throne room where Lord Devon was sitting and talking to a young woman. The woman was dressed in a rather bright tunic and a long leather skirt.

"I wanted to introduce you to our new council person. This is Evelyn," Lord Devon said to Keals.

"It is nice to meet you," Evelyn said.

"No, the pleasure is all mine," Keals said taking Evelyn's right hand and kissed it.

"Come; let us go to the courtyard. Bella will be arriving in a few moments," Lord Devon said.

The three of them left the throne room and walked to the main courtyard. The councilpersons and a group of servants began to gather around. Just then a messenger announced Queen Bella's arrival, moments later the royal carriage pulled up. A guard opened the door and Bella slowly climbed out of the carriage, she kissed Devon and smiled.

"It is so good to be back home," Bella said, and then she turned to the awaiting audience. "Thank you all for coming to welcome me home."

Bella and Devon held each other's hands and went inside.

"Would you like a personal showing of the castle from me?" Keals asked Evelyn.

"I would like that very much," she replied.

"Would you mind terribly if I held your hand?" Keals asked.

"No, I do not mind at all," Evelyn answered.

Just then they went inside hand and hand. As the tour progressed, they started talking and getting to know each other. They ended up at Keals' quarters; they held each other's hands again and went inside the quarters. An hour later Keals came out of his quarters buttoning up his shirt, Evelyn smiled at him and left. After Queen Bella's welcome home supper banquet, Keals and Evelyn went to the garden together, and Devon and Bella went to their quarters.

The following morning at the farm Cheats was chasing around butterflies happily, while Isaiah and Liza were doing chores. Minutes later Boby rode up on the wagon and unloaded some provisions, and Liza and

Isaiah brought them inside. Isaiah played with Cheats as Liza made lunch. After lunch Brandon, Madison and their parents came over. They sat around talking and hung out for the rest of the day. The sun slowly went down and they left the farm leaving Isaiah and his parents to finish the chores.

The very next day in the castle, after breakfast, Keals and Evelyn were in Keals' quarters holding hands and talking, moments later Evelyn left the quarters. All of a sudden, the Black Shadow appeared to Keals. The Black Shadow stared at him with glowing eyes as Keals stared back with a blank look on his face.

"So, have you decided to help us or not?" the Black Shadow asked.

"Yes, I have, and I will help you," Keals answered blankly. "But what will I have to do?"

"You will just have to follow our instructions," the Black Shadow said.

"And this is all for the good of Old York New, right?" Keals questioned.

"I can assure you this is all for the greater good," the Black Shadow replied with a smirk. "You must bring me a body. I must have solid form to go on any farther."

Just then Keals left the room and went to the council room entrance; there were two guards in front of the closed door. Keals opened the door and they went in, one of the councilpersons was in the room. He was sitting at the table reading some parchments. Suddenly ice-cold air filled the room, and an invisible Black Shadow came. The two guards and the councilman felt an unnatural deathly presence, and they slowly backed up into a corner. The Black Shadow glided closer and closer, the three persons became more scared as the unnatural evil force closed in on them. All of a sudden, the Black Shadow appeared to them; the three humans stood dead still frozen in horror. The creature was inches away from the guards and councilman when the Black Shadow squeezed itself into his mouth. The councilman's eyeballs rolled backwards and he fell to the ground screaming in agony.

Moments later his eyes shot open with glowing fiery yellow eyes. As all this was unfolding Keals stood there, staring, in a hypnotic trance. The Black Shadow smiled a wide smirk as it tested its newly possessed body. He bobbed its head from side to side and its tongue shot in and out like a serpent. The Black Shadow walked over to the two guards and touched their faces. Both guards screamed in agony and combusted into flames. The demon walked over to Keals and smiled a large smirk at him.

"I'm Supay. You're glad to be in my presence," the Black Shadow in the councilman's body said. "Now, you must put an end to Queen Bella's reign."

"Must we? What is the real purpose?" Keals asked curiously.

"Because she'll start Devon's evilness," Supay answered. "We'll come to you with further instructions."

Just then the Black Shadow left the room leaving Keals alone.

Back at the farm Isaiah and Cheats were running around outside playing. Week by week Cheats got bigger and stronger and now he was double the size from when they found him. Liza called them in for lunch so they both ran into the cabin. As Isaiah ate he fed Cheats some meat from off his plate. When they both were done eating, they went back outside. As the evening approached Isaiah, his parents, and Cheats laid down in the field and watched as the sun went down.

The moon shined brightly in the night sky and the stars twinkled high above Old York New. Deep inside the castle garden, a large cauldron was bubbling away on top of a large cracking fire. A cloaked figure was chanting aloud as he stirred the thick black bubbling liquid in the cauldron. The cloaked figure was wearing a long black leather robe. Just then the figure let down its hood; it was Supay. Supay added berries, herbs, and dried mushroom to the cauldron as it chanted even louder. Just then he ladled the bubbling liquid into a small vial and secured it with a stopper. He slipped the vial into his pocket, and then put his hood back on and left the garden.

The following day after breakfast Brandon, Madison, and their parents came to the farm for a visit. Cheats and the kids played outside as their parents talked inside the cabin. Cheats jumped into a tree and climbed higher and higher and the children followed him. A little while later Ruth and little Scottie came over, so the children jumped out of the tree and greeted them.

"How are you doing my children?" Ruth asked.

"We are doing good," Isaiah replied.

"Are your parents home?" Ruth asked.

"Yeah. They are inside talking to Anna and Joseph," he replied.

She went into the cabin and the kids continued to play with Cheats.

"Why have you not been around?" Isaiah asked.

"Mother has not let me out alone ever since we saw the Black Shadows in town," Scottie replied.

"How is everything with you and your mother since that day?" Madison asked.

"Well, Mother is still keeping ever vigilant, but she is getting better," Scottie answered. "But it still feels strange."

A little while later, Anna called them in for lunch; they had beef and mushroom stew. After they were finished eating, the children went back outside and played. An hour later the visitors left leaving Isaiah and his parents alone. Liza came out and began playing with Isaiah and Cheats. Later that day in the castle Evelyn and Keals were in the garden holding hands and talking. Just then Supay came up to them and greeted them.

"I must speak to Keals in private," Supay said.

"I must also speak with you so I will see you later," Evelyn said.

She kissed Keals on the cheek and left.

"I see you have been enjoying her," Supay said with a smirk.

"It is not like that. I really like her," Keals said.

Supay pulled out the small clear vial with dark liquid in it.

"Tonight, at supper, pour this into Queen Bella's wine. And make sure she drinks every last drop," Supay said.

"What is this?" Keals asked.

"Do not worry about it," the Black Shadow replied, "and make sure nobody sees you."

"Okay," Keals said.

He took the vial, slipped it into his pocket, and walked away.

Keals went to the throne room where Devon and Bella were sitting on the throne talking with a councilperson.

The councilperson left and Lord Devon began talking with him. A little later Keals left the throne room and went back to his quarters. He sat at his work table and began thinking. Minutes later there was a knock at the door so he opened it, it was Evelyn. She greeted him with a kiss and came inside.

"Can you sit down? I have something important to tell you," Evelyn said.

"What is it? Is everything okay?" Keals asked.

"I am with child. I am having your child," Evelyn said.

"Are you sure it is mine?" Keals asked.

"You are the only one I have ever been with," Evelyn answered.

Keals sat on his bed wide-eyed; he quickly looked up at Evelyn and smiled.

"This is wonderful news. I am truly happy," Keals said.

He stood up again and gave Evelyn a long kiss.

"When did you find out?" Keals asked excitedly.

"Just this past day," Evelyn answered.

Just then Keals bent down and kissed her stomach.

"Did you tell anyone else yet?"

"No, not yet."

"I do not think you should tell anyone just yet.

"Why is that?"

"I just think we should wait a while."

"Okay if that is what you wish."

They kissed each other again and left the room.

The day drew on slowly turning into evening. The smells of supper being made filled the air. Keals went to the dining hall and found a servant setting the tables. He told the servant to bring two jugs of wine, so the servant left the room. Keals walked to Devon and Bella's seats. He took the vial out of his pocket and poured every drop of liquid into one of the cups, and then he slipped the empty vial back into his pocket. Just then the servant came back with two wine jugs. Keals took one of the jugs and started filling up Devon and Bella's chalices with wine.

"Sir, let me do that," the servant said.

"No, I insist I help you," Keals said.

Moments later Devon, Bella, and the others entered the dining hall, everyone sat down and the servants started bringing food to them. They ate, laughed, and drank not knowing what had just taken place. Minutes slipped into hours and the supper feast had finally ended. The people washed up and left as the servants came and cleaned up. Keals and Evelyn held hands and went to Keals' quarters. During that night Queen Bella slept uneasily, breathing heavily with difficulty.

Devon being a very heavy deep sleeper hadn't known what was unfolding. Around midnight, Queen Bella struggled for her last breath and with that the life extinguished from her body.

The night slowly went by and morning finally came. Devon woke up and gave Bella a gentle kiss on her lips. When she hadn't woken up, he softly shook her. Realizing she was cold, Devon screamed for help. For several long moments, everything seemed to be frozen in suspended animation. Moments later two guards came and quickly carried Bella's body to the infirmary. Devon quickly followed behind them and waited outside the infirmary doors. Minutes later a nurse maiden approached him and told him she had passed away, tears rolled down his face as he wept bitterly. He went into the infirmary to Bella's lifeless body and wept even louder over the body. Throughout the day people came up to Lord Devon to express their condolences. That evening, Lord Devon went to his quarters without eating and cried himself to sleep.

The next morning Devon woke up early, got ready, and began making preparations for Bella's burial. It was a dark and rainy day, messengers and the guards went door to door telling people about the death of Bella and about her burial.

Back at the farm Ruth and Scottie appeared at the door of the cabin. Isaiah greeted them with a hug, and the three of them went inside. They all sat down for breakfast and ate and talked.

"Did the guards come yet?" Ruth asked.

"Why would they come here?" Liza asked.

"Wow, you honestly do not know yet? I thought everybody knew," Ruth answered surprisingly. "Queen Bella died last night."

Isaiah and his parent's mouths dropped down; they were wide-eyed and in shock.

"Her burial is morrow morning," Scottie added.

When they were done eating, Cheats and the children went outside and played while their parents stayed inside and continued talking. A little while later Ruth and little Scottie left, leaving Isaiah and his parents to do the farm chores. Some time had passed and a messenger came by and told them about Queen Bella. The day went by unusually slowly, and after supper they went straight to bed.

The morning of the burial was cold and very cloudy. Isaiah and his parents got ready in their

Sunday's best and left the cabin. Boby hitched the wagon to the horses, and then they got on and rode away. They stopped at the cottage to pick up Ruth and Scottie and rode to the castle. The castle's chapel was so packed that they had to stand in the back. After the service people began lining up to view Bella's body. An hour later a group of monks carried Bella's body to the burial yard. They placed the wrapped-up body into a freshly dug hole, people came and dropped handfuls of dirt into the hole.

Slowly the people began leaving the castle. Liza and Boby dropped Ruth and Scottie back home and went to the farm. It stayed rainy and cloudy, and all of Old York New was somber for the rest of the day. Isaiah fed Cheats and helped his parents with the farm chores. Back at the castle, it was very unusually quiet. Devon was in his quarters, sitting on his bed, weeping bitterly. Just then there was a knock at the door, so he opened it, it was a servant.

"Supper is ready," the servant said.

"I am not hungry," Devon said.

"But you must eat something," the servant said.

"I do not want anything to eat!"

"I am sorry to bother you," the servant softly said leaving the room.

Devon grabbed a glass chalice off his nightstand and threw it; it hit the wall and shattered into pieces. He knelt on the floor and started picking up the glass shards. All of a sudden, he got cut on a shard of glass. It felt good to bleed, really good. For days Devon felt that his life and all this had been a dream. One horrible nightmare he so wanted to wake up from. He tore up a bed sheet and wrapped up his cut-up hand. Then he dropped to his knees by his bed and started crying again.

Meanwhile in Keals' quarters, Evelyn and Keals were holding each other's hands; smiling. Evelyn felt guilty for being unusually happy so she left the room. Just then there was a knock on the door, so he opened it thinking that Evelyn had returned, but it was Supay. He entered and Keals quickly closed the door behind him.

"What are you doing here?" Keals asked bitterly.

"I wanted to let you know that we're going to go ahead with the next step of our plan," Supay said.

"What are you going to do, kill Devon like you killed Queen Bella?" Keals exclaimed in anger "Why did you not tell me you were going to kill the Queen?"

"First of all, you're the one who killed Bella. I simply gave you the tool to do so," Supay flatly said.

"I cannot help you anymore. I cannot kill any more people," Keals said.

"Like I told you, this is all for the greater good. And besides, we're not going to kill your Lord Devon," Supay hissed with a smirk. "We have other plans for him. Just be ready at night in two days' time."

Just then Supay left the quarters and Keals laid on his bed and thought for a while. Evening finally came and everyone had supper and with full stomachs went to sleep.

Chapter 6
The Poisoned Elixir

The following morning at the farm they woke up at sunrise and Isaiah began his chores. A little later Ruth and Scottie came over and Liza and Boby invited them to have breakfast with them. As they ate they talked. Ruth asked to borrow the wagon to pick up their provisions and Liza said yes. Ruth thanked them and she and Scottie went to the stable. As Ruth hitched the wagon to the horses, Isaiah came to them and said Liza gave him permission to go with them. So, they got on the wagon and rode away. When they got to town, Ruth tied up the horses.

"Can I go visit Uncle Lenn at his shop?" Isaiah asked.

"Yes, you may," Ruth replied.

"May I go with Isaiah?" Scottie asked.

"Of course, you may. I will walk you both there," Ruth answered.

Isaiah's uncle was a steelworks man, and his shop was in the center of town. When they got to his shop, sparks were flying everywhere. There was a man working with melted steel. He was slightly taller than Isaiah, and he was wearing protective wear. Just then he looked up and smiled wide. He came over to them; he shook Ruth and Scottie's hands and gave Isaiah a hug.

"How are you my boy? How are your parents?" the man asked.

"I am fine Lenn papa, Mother is doing fine and you know Father," Isaiah replied.

"We all know your Father," Lenn replied with a scowl.

"Why have you not come and visited us for a while Lenn papa?"

"Because I have been very busy. I have a large order for swords from Lord Devon," Lenn replied.

"Hi Lenn, how are you doing?" Ruth asked.

"Besides being very busy, I am doing very good. How are you doing Ruth?"

"I am doing good."

"Can we stay with Lenn papa for a while?" Isaiah asked.

"It is up to Lenn. But if he says it is okay, then it is fine by me," Ruth said.

"Of course, you can stay if you want," Lenn said.

"Thanks so much," the boys said.

"I will be back right after I get the provision," Ruth said.

Then she smiled at Lenn and kissed him on the cheek.

"Thank you so much."

"You are very welcome," Lenn said with a smile.

Just then Ruth left them and Lenn turned to the boys.

"Do you two want to help me?" Lenn asked.

"That would be cool," the boys replied.

Lenn gave them protective goggles and aprons and the boys put them on. Just then Lenn poured a line of bubbling liquid metal on a work stone. When the metal was cool enough, he took a hammer and banged it out, fashioning the metal into a sword. The boys helped by putting the finished swords in piles. After a while Lenn let the boys pour the melted liquid metal onto the work stone. An hour later Ruth came back, so they said farewell to Lenn and left the shop. Ruth had already put the things on the wagon, so they got on the wagon and left. When they got to the cottage, they unloaded the provisions, and they left again.

When they got to the farm, Ruth unhitched the wagon and put the horses in the stable. Liza greeted them and Cheats came over and started chasing Isaiah around. They went inside, sat at the dining table, and talked about their day. Liza told Ruth and Scottie to stay for lunch so the boys set the table. For lunch, they had rice and beef with spices. A little while later Boby came in carrying a sack over his shoulders.

"Hey father, where did you go?" Isaiah asked.

"I had to pick up a few things from town," Boby answered.

"Why did you not just let me know what you needed?" Ruth asked.

"Because I needed the walk," Boby replied.

"Anyway, we are going. Thank you again for lunch," Ruth said.

She and little Scottie hugged everyone, bid them farewell and left.

Afternoon slowly drifted by turning into evening, the castle's atmosphere was tranquil and quiet. The only sounds were low murmuring coming from deep in the castle's garden. There was a group of hooded cloaked figures murmuring low and steadily. The hooded group raised their arms into the air and started chanting in hissed voices. The figure at the head of the group raised its hood, it was Supay.

"Do you think Keals will find out our true plans?" a person asked.

"No, that fool is too stupid to find out," Supay answered with a hiss "And besides, by the time he does he'll be under our full control."

Just then the demon chuckled evilly; they slipped their hood back on and continued chanting.

As the night went on the chanting became louder and sounded more and more demonic. The following morning Keals woke up early and got ready for the day. Just then there was a low knock at the door, the door opened and Evelyn came in. Keals kissed her, and bent down and kissed her stomach.

"How was your night?" Keals asked.

"I slept very well. Thank you," Evelyn replied.

They both walked hand and hand to the dining hall. When they were done eating, they went to the garden. All of a sudden, Supay came up and bowed at them.

"I must talk to Keals."

"I will see you later," Evelyn said.

She bowed to both of them and slowly left.

"We are ready for the next step of our plan," Supay said.

"What must I do?" Keals asked.

Supay took out a clear vial with blue liquid from his pocket and handed it to Keals.

"Pour a few drops of this liquid into Devon's drink each night," Supay said.

"What is this elixir for?" Keals asked worriedly. "This looks like the thing that killed Queen Bella."

"Don't worry, it won't kill him. It'll just make him see the truth," Supay answered. "And remember only give him a couple of drops."

Keals bowed to Supay and they both left the garden. Keals went to the throne room, guards saluted him and he went into the room. Devon was talking with all the council members, Evelyn looked up and smiled at Keals. Just then Lord Devon saw Keals, so he took him aside and spoke with him. A little later Keals had left the throne room and went to his quarters.

Moments later Evelyn came to the room and they sat on the bed and talked. Evelyn told him that she was getting worried about his actions and that started an argument. Tears rolled down Evelyn's cheeks and she left the room upset. Keals wanted to follow her but he thought it best to let her emotions cool down. As evening approached everyone went to the dining hall for supper.

After eating, Keals went to the kitchen; he grabbed a chalice and a bottle of milk and went back to the dining hall. He took the vial out of his pocket, poured a couple of drops of the elixir into the chalice, and slipped it back into his pocket. He poured some milk into the chalice and took it to Devon's quarters. He knocked on the door and Devon opened it.

"Yes Keals, what can I do for you?" Devon asked.

"Here is your evening cup of milk," Keals said.

"I do not want it," Devon said flatly.

"Before she passed away Queen Bella made me promise to take care of you. And that is what I intend to do," Keals said handing Devon the cup.

Devon drained the milk in two gulps and handed the chalice back.

"Thank you," Devon said with a slight smile.

"You are welcome," Keals said and he walked away.

As the night, progressed Lord Devon tossed and turned from strange dreams he had. The days slowly passed by and things at the castle were quiet and uneventful.

One morning, the kids got up and got ready for the day. Brandon and Madison helped Isaiah and his parents with the farm chores. After doing their chores, the children played with Cheats. At midafternoon Liza dropped Brandon and Madison back home. One of their cows were about to give birth, so Isaiah and Boby stood there at the ready in case the cow needed help during the birth. Liza came back home just in time to see the birth of two healthy male calves. Liza and Boby cleaned the baby calves and the calves went to their mother for milk. A little later they started their evening chores.

It was late evening, a bright full moon was out, and the stars were twinkling high above Old York New. Everything was very quiet in the castle. Devon was in his quarters laying down on his bed and thinking. In Keals' quarters, Keals was looking over some parchments at his table. All of a sudden, there was a knock at the door; Supay came into the room.

"We see that you've been giving Devon the elixir," Supay said.

"Except for today. I have given a few drops of the elixir in some milk every night," Keals said.

"Why haven't you given him the elixir tonight?" the demon asked, "You mustn't miss giving him the poisoned elixir for a single day."

"Okay, as you command," Keals said.

Just then they both left the room.

Days slowly passed and the elixir started to take its effects on Lord Devon. Day by day Devon was slowly driven crazily insane until he finally cracked. He started talking to himself and to people who were not really there. One-day Ruth and Scottie were in town when they saw Devon and Keals. They saw Devon talking to himself and attacking strange. Ruth went over to them and asked what happened to Lord Devon. Keals told them that Devon had become ill ever since the death of Queen Bella. Just then Ruth and Scottie left and continued their shopping. It slowly turned into noon and the town began getting more and more crowded with people.

At midafternoon Ruth and Scottie finished their shopping so they left town and slowly walked to their cottage. They put away the stuff they purchased and left their cottage again. They moved away from the cottage and teleported. Moments later they appeared in front of Liza and Boby's farm. Isaiah and Cheats were playing outside so Isaiah greeted them and they went inside.

"Hello friends, how are you doing?" Ruth asked them.

"We are doing good," Liza replied.

"We have news for you. Devon has fallen ill," Ruth said to them.

"How do you know this?" Liza asked.

"Because we saw him in town and he was talking to himself and acting strange," Ruth answered. "Keals said he was driven ill from the death of Queen Bella but I do not know if that is the truth."

They talked for a while and a little while later Ruth and Scottie left.

Chapter 7
The New Person in Charge

The following day after breakfast Keals helped Devon back to his room. Keals went to his quarters, moments later Evelyn came to the room and they talked for a while. A little while later Evelyn left the room. Just then there was a knock at the door and Supay walked into the room. He talked to Keals as he stared blankly into his eyes. Moment later Supay left the room. The morning slowly turned into noon and everyone went to the dining hall for lunch.

Meanwhile in town things were strangely quiet and empty. It was unusual because this time was the busiest of the day. The Black Shadow walked up to a group of people. It spoke to the group trying to convince them to become their followers. More and more people came to Supay, curious about what it had to say. People were amazed at how he was speaking about Devon. Some people listened to what he had to say, others would not have any of it and were in full support of Lord Devon.

Back at the castle, Evelyn and the other council persons were discussing things. Just then Evelyn called for a messenger and told him to go get Keals and Supay. A couple of minutes later the messenger got to town and informed Supay that the other council members needed him so they left town. When they got to the castle, they retrieved Keals from his quarters and met the others in the council room. Keals and the council members sat and began talking.

"We are here to discuss the situation with Lord Devon," Evelyn said.

"Day by day Devon's illness is making his mental capacity digresses," one of the council members said, "at this rate, he will not be able to lead Old York New by the next full moon."

"Maybe Lord Devon will get better soon," Evelyn said.

"I don't think he'll get better. I think Keals should take over for Devon," Supay said.

"Why do you sound different?" Evelyn asked.

"I am not feeling well," Supay quickly answered with a cough.

"Why do you bother him with such frivolous inquires? The point is he is right, Keals should take over for Lord Devon until such a time where he can take up the throne again," a councilperson Tier said.

"All in favor for Keals to take over for Lord Devon raise your hands," Sir Tier called out.

All the council members except for Keals, Evelyn and three others raised their hands.

"Then it is unanimous. Keals will become ruler," Sir Tier announced.

Just then they left the council room and Supay took Keals aside.

"Congratulations to you 'Lord Keals,'" the demon said.

"Thank you," Keals said with a smirk.

"Why didn't you raise your hand when they asked?" Supay asked.

"It would have looked bad," Keals replied. "Anyway, I will talk to you later."

They both parted ways and Keals went back to his quarters. He was about to lie down when there was a knock at the door, and he answered it, it was Evelyn.

"I just came to say congratulations," Evelyn said.

"Thank you," Keals replied. "Why did you not raise your hand when they asked?"

"To be honest. I think Lord Devon will get well soon," Evelyn said. "Are you happy? Do you think you will be a good king?"

"I really do not know," Keals replied.

Both of them smiled; kissed each other and laid down.

Sir Tier and the other council members were making arrangements for Keals' coronation ceremony. The monks were told to make plans for it also. The cooks were told to prepare a supper feast for the coronation ceremony. Evelyn had left Keals' quarters and Keals sat at his table and began writing a speech on some parchment. Messengers and guards were sent door to door to tell everyone that in two days' time was Keals coronation as the new king. People were shocked to hear the news about Lord Devon and Keals.

Meanwhile at the farm, Madison, Brandon, and their parents had come for a visit. Isaiah, Madison, Brandon, and Cheats were outside playing while their parents were inside talking. All of a sudden, Ruth and Scottie appeared outside the cabin. The children greeted them both and Ruth went inside. Cheats and the children played a little while longer and went inside. Moments later they heard horses outside and there was a knock at the door. Liza curiously opened the door, it was a royal messenger. He informed them that the coronation of Keals was in two days' time and then he left. For a while, they all talked about Keals and Devon. After supper the visitors left, leaving Isaiah and his parents alone to do the chores.

It was finally the day of the coronation and the castle was hustling and bustling with busyness. The monks were going over things while flower arrangements were being set up. Most of the council members were in the council room discussing today's affairs. Keals was in his quarters pacing back and forth going over his speech. Evelyn was with him trying to relax him.

"Do not worry, you will do just fine," Evelyn said.

"I am not worried. In fact, I am feeling fine," Keals replied with a smile.

Just then there was a loud knock at the door and Keals answered it, it was Supay.

"It's time, we must go," he said.

They slowly left the room and made their way to the castle chapel. When they got to the chapel, it was empty except for the monks and the council members. Slowly crowds of people started to fill the chapel. When every last seat was finally filled, the ceremony began.

"We are all here for the crowning ceremony of our new king, Keals of Niyon. Will you solemnly promise and swear to govern the people of Old York New and of your possessions and territories to any belonging or pertaining, according to their true laws and customs?" the monks asked.

"I solemnly promise to do so," Keals answered.

"Will you to your power cause law and justice, in mercy, to be executed in all your judgment?" the monks farther asked.

"I solemnly promise to do so," Keals answered

"Will you to the utmost of your power maintain the laws of God with true profession? Will you maintain and preserve inviolable the settlement of the church of Old York New established in Old York New?" the monks finally said.

"All this I promise to do. The things which I have here before promised, I will perform and keep. So, help me God," Keals answered.

"Then, by the powers that are invested in us from God above, I dub thee the new King of Old York New."

The other monk took a sword and tapped both Keals' shoulders with it, then the monks turned to the people.

"By the powers from above we pronounce you our new king, Lord Keals," both monks said.

One of the monks placed the crown on Keals' head and everyone clapped their hands. Just then Keals took out the piece of parchment, unfolded it, and started giving the speech, after his speech everyone clapped once again. After the ceremony, some people stayed for the supper banquet while others left. For the feast, there were platters of roasted pig and turkey, and many varieties of stuffing. There were bowls full of cranberry chutney and roasted mushrooms, and for dessert there were pies and tarts of many kinds. An hour later the feast had ended and the people started leaving.

When they got home Brandon, Madison and their parents went to sleep. For the next few days, the cool fall air became cooler and cooler in Old York New. Day by day Keals' soul got darker and darker until his physical self was affected. The whites of his eyes took on a yellowish tone, and tiny blood vessels also appeared around his eyes. His facial features became slightly distorted. Meanwhile at the farm, Liza and Boby started storing the vegetation for the winter.

One morning Isaiah woke up, fed Cheats, and did his chores. After his chores, he got permission to go to Brandon and Madison's home. They both greeted him outside the cottage and the three of them went inside and talked. Just then they heard horses outside, and Joseph and Anna came and gave the kids hugs. They all sat down and began to talk.

"What do you think about Keals being our new king?" Isaiah asked.

"I think it was a big mistake making him ruler," Anna replied.

"I think most of Old York New feels the same way," Joseph said.

"Do you think Lord Devon will ever get well?" Brandon asked.

"Well, let us hope that Lord Devon gets well soon," Anna said.

They talked for a while longer and the kids went outside.

Meanwhile at the castle, Evelyn and Keals were spending time with each other. Evelyn's pregnant stomach was beginning to show, and she was absolutely glowing. She was starting to notice the change in Keals' appearance and demeanor. Evelyn started talking about Supay, which started another argument between them. Evelyn quickly got up and left the room with tears in her eyes. Keals was totally oblivious to his dark side so he did not realize she was right.

Suddenly there was a knock at the door and a messenger walked in and informed him that Supay wanted to talk to him, and they both left the room. As the day passed by Keals spent it with the Black Shadow. It had convinced Keals to make all the people of Old York New wear different color tunics to establish the different social classes of people. Slowly evening arrived and everyone in the castle had supper and went to sleep.

The days passed slowly and as Keals spend more and more time with the Black Shadow his dark side got worse. It was a Sunday when Keals sent out a request for the people of Old York New to come for a public assembly. Meanwhile in town the Black Shadows were being spotted. They didn't possess anyone but they were wreaking havoc, tempting people to do horrible almost evil things they wouldn't normally do.

Evelyn and Keals hadn't talked or seen each other in days. Evelyn was in the council room looking over some documents when there was a knock at the door. Evelyn curiously went to the door and opened it, Keals smiled at her and walked in. He apologized to her without really meaning it; she thanked him and kissed him. Minutes later a messenger came and told them that people were there for the public assembly.

They slowly made their way to the main courtyard. There was a large group of people for the meeting, and the council members were standing on a slightly elevated platform. Isaiah and his parents, Brandon, Madison, and their parents, and little Scottie and Ruth were in the back of the crowd. Suddenly Keals began speaking.

"I have come to understand that many of you do not like the fact that I am your new king. Others have certain reservations towards me," Keals began to announce. "This means that you are against me, which means you are against Old York New as well."

Keals called over three councilmembers to him.

"Are you against me?" Keals asked.

"We are not against you, we just think it was wrong, how you became king we mean," one of the councilmembers said.

"I will no longer be requiring your services," Keals said.

Keals and Supay took out daggers and plunged them in the chest of two councilmen twisting them around. The third councilman tried to run but Supay grabbed him by the throat and forced him to the ground, and Supay put him in shackles.

"Like I said, if you are not with me then you are against me and Old York New," Keals called out loud. "And from this day forth, all of you people will address me as Lord Keals."

Evelyn, with astonishment and fear, ran from Keals' side. Just then guards grabbed the shackled-up councilman; the two lifeless bodies and dragged them away. The crowd was left shocked by the events that just unfolded.

Chapter 8
Plans and Preparations

The harsh and bitter frozen air of the winter took its toll on the crops on Liza and Boby's farm. A crackling fire was set ablaze in the fireplace; Isaiah, Liza, and Boby were handled by the fire playing with Cheats. A few hours later Liza and Boby went to feed the farm animals and Isaiah did his chores. When Liza came back inside, she started making supper. Later Isaiah set the table and they began eating; for dinner they had rice and beef stew. When they were done eating, they said their prayers and went to sleep. The frozen night air blew so heavily that it nearly cracked the windows.

The following morning as they were having breakfast they heard horses outside, Cheats ran to the door and began scratching at it. Liza went and answered the door; it was Anna, Brandon, Madison, and Joseph. Liza closed the door behind them, she dished some food up for the visitors, and they all ate and talked. After breakfast, the children played with Cheats while their parent talked.

Meanwhile at the castle, Keals was getting worried about Evelyn. She had been neglecting her duties as councilwoman, she hadn't been seen at the castle or around town either ever since the public assembly. Keals had sent word to Evelyn's parents' house with a messenger hawk but hadn't received word back. At this point, Lord Devon was getting progressively worse, mentally, from the poisoned elixir he was given.

At the castle burial yard, there were pools of blood leading up to the garden entrance. Supay was feasting on children. There were children tied up in a large catacomb building, they were screaming and crying for help. There were torn up bloody carcasses littered all over; fresh blood was dripping down from the Black Shadow's mouth. The demon slowly walked to the catacombs with glowing eyes. He snarled and gnawed in hunger, he howled at the full moon and the kids screamed for their lives.

Back at Ruth's cottage Ruth and Scottie were watching the sun go down and the moon rise. Ruth went inside, grabbed a key off the hook, and went outside again. Little Scottie followed her to the stable and they went to the back. Ruth inserted the key into a hole and turned it, a little door opened revealing a combination look wheel. She turned the wheel around four times and a part of the wall clicked open. Ruth lifted up the opened wall to reveal a small pile of gold coins and old looking books.

"I did not know this was here," Scottie said.

"Well, before your father had passed away he made this for me to protect my books and other things," Ruth began explaining. "You see Scottie, in some parts of the world, witches, sorceresses, and people of magic are hunted and some are even killed."

"Mother, why do you never talk about father?" Scottie asked.

"Because it still makes me sad to talk about him," Ruth replied as tears rolled down her cheeks.

She wiped away her tears and smiled at Scottie.

"Can you help me with these books," Ruth asked.

"Yeah, I will," Scottie replied.

They grabbed the books and took them inside, placing them on the dining table.

"I will be back, I have to close the storage door," Ruth said.

Moments later Ruth came back and began opening up the books.

"What are we looking for?" Scottie asked.

"Answers. Keals was acting strange, and he also looked strange. I have a feeling about something but I must do some enquiry to see if I am correct," Ruth replied.

"You said that we should never use Black Witchcraft. Then why do you have books on black witchcraft?" Scottie asked.

"It is true that you and I should never use black witchcraft, we must only use White Witchcraft. But I have these books in case I must do research in black witchcraft," Ruth replied.

Then they started their research. After many cups of tea and a long sleepless night, they found what Ruth was looking for.

"Thank you for all your help. Now go get some sleep," Ruth said kissing Scottie's forehead.

He smiled and kissed Ruth and went to his room.

Meanwhile at the castle, everyone was just waking up. The only light in the castle was coming from a few candles. Keals got more and more scared for Evelyn's health and her whereabouts so after breakfast he sent out a search party to look for Evelyn. As the morning drew on reports of missing children, livestock and strange howling sounds at night came flooding into Keals. Keals had a bad feeling of what was going on but he didn't want to believe his conscious.

A few hours later at the cottage, Ruth and Scottie woke up from their sleep and changed their clothes. They left the cottage and Ruth locked the door behind herself, they moved a distance away and teleported.

They both popped out of thin air in front of Liza and Boby's farm. Cheats was outside chasing round butterflies; all of a sudden, he looked up and saw them. He ran over to them; jumped on them and began licking their faces. They got up and went inside. Isaiah and his parents greeted them and they sat down.

"Remember what I was talking about the other day? Well, I was right," Ruth said.

"What are you talking about?" Liza asked.

"About something being really wrong with Keals. According to the enquiry Scottie and I did Keals has been exposed to a truly evil entity for a very long period of time," Ruth started to explain, "and it all adds up since the appearance of the Black Shadows in Old York New."

"Are you sure about all of this?" Liza asked.

"I am very positive," Ruth answered. "I also have more material on the Black Shadows."

"What did you find out about them?" Boby asked.

"Well, firstly, the Black Shadows are actually Demons. They are the most malevolent and most powerful under Lucifer's ruling," Ruth started to explain. "The Black Shadows are also the guardians of the gates of the underworld, of Hell itself."

"But can anyone in Keals' presence actually be possessed? And who may they be?" Liza asked.

"I do not know, but there might be a way we can find out," Ruth said.

"What are you up to today?" Liza asked.

"I am going to town to take care of something," Ruth replied.

"If your parents would let you, would you and Cheats like to spend the night at my home?" Scottie asked.

"That would be cool," Isaiah replied and he turned to Liza. "May I spend the night at their house?"

"Of course, you can," Liza replied.

Isaiah went to his room and packed a cloth sack with his clothes.

"Bye Mother, bye Father. I will see you morrow," Isaiah said kissing Liza and Boby.

Just then Isaiah, Ruth, and Scottie left the farm and slowly walked up the field, and Cheats trailed behind them. When they got to the cottage, Ruth went to the stable and opened the secret storage, grabbed some bottles and herbs and closed the door again. She told the boys that she was going to go to town and she would be back in a while. She hugged the boys and quickly left the cottage.

About an hour later she got to town and went to a tavern. The tavern innkeeper greeted her and led her to a room in the back. Ruth sat on the ground and made a protective circle around herself with a bottle of salt, and lit candles around the circle. She took off her pentagram necklace and placed herbs in the middle of the circle. Just then Ruth began to chant as he slowly spun the necklace around the herbs.

All of a sudden, a breeze blew through the room and a mist appeared from out of the herbs. The mist changed colors, from black to gray, and finally to a bright blue. She was disappointed by what she had seen so she packed everything into her cloth sack and left the room. Ruth thanked the tavern innkeeper, bid him farewell and left. She walked through town browsing through things and thinking. Why hadn't the spell she cast worked? It had worked the other times she had cast it, so why not this time? She went to this little shack looking shop and purchase some more herbs and potions.

When Ruth was done with her shopping, she made her way to the castle. When she got to the gate, she smiled at the guards and they let her in. Moments later she reached the throne room, the guards opened the door and she went in. Supay and Keals were standing around talking. Keals looked strange and sounded even stranger.

"Hello Lord Keals, I just stopped by to see how Lord Devon is doing," Ruth said.

"He is doing fine. He went to his quarters to retire early," Keals replied.

"Who is he?" Ruth asked.

"This is my council member Supay," Keals replied.

"I am just going to come out and say it," Ruth said softly. "You are acting strange. What is wrong?"

"Nothing is wrong with him," Supay said.

"First, I did not ask you, I asked Lord Keals. Secondly, it is not right answering other people's questions for them," Ruth said.

"How dare you talk to me like that!" Supay exclaimed.

Just then Keals raised his hand and they stopped talking.

"You will not talk to us like that witch," Keals said.

"But…" Ruth said.

Keals raised his hand once again.

"You have a son, right? How is he doing?" Keals asked softly "You would not want anything bad happening to him."

"Well, I am sorry for bothering you. Tell Lord Devon I asked for him," Ruth said.

"I will," Keals said.

Ruth quickly left the throne room and the guards closed the door behind her.

"Do you think she knows that you are the Black Shadow?" Keals asked.

"I don't think that the fleshling knows," Supay said.

Ruth ran out of town and quickly made her way home. When she got back to the cottage, she grabbed the children and they teleported to the farm. The teleportation took a lot out of Ruth so she rested by the stable for a little while. Minutes later Isaiah unlocked the door and they went inside. Ruth asked for water and Liza gave her a canteen of water. Ruth took the canteen, drained it in two gulps, and handed it back.

"So, I know who the Black Shadow is. It is the male councilmember," Ruth began to explain. "And the demon's name is Supay."

'How did you find out?" Liza asked.

"Well I tried to cast a spell but it did not work, I think he is blocking all types of detection spells. I also felt his aura and he is more powerful than I thought," Ruth said.

"What are we going to do?" Liza asked.

"I think we should start a rebellion. Most of the people in Old York New do not like Keals as our new king," Ruth began to say. "If we band together as one, we have a chance to get rid of Keals and get Lord

Devon back on the throne. We also must help Lord Devon because I believe Keals did something to him."

They left the kids and Cheats behind and left the cabin. Boby hitched the wagon to the horses, and they got on and rode away. They picked up Joseph and Anna from their home and left. They explained everything to Anna and Joseph as they rode to town. When they got to town, Liza tied the horses up and they left. They went door to door to the supporters of Lord Devon and let them know they were having an assembly in the field by Liza and Boby's farm. Ruth went to the tavern and told the innkeeper to inform the other white witches of Old York New about the assembly.

The moon was shining brightly high above the land. They untied the horses, got on the wagon, and left town. When they got to their homes, they went to sleep. Meanwhile at the castle's burial yard, there was a group of seventy of the Black Shadows' followers. They were chanting in high demonic voices. Suddenly they all lowered their hoods. Standing in front of the group just below the Black Shadow stood Keals.

The following morning at the farm after the chores and breakfast, they began getting prepared for the assembly. As the day drew on Ruth and Scottie came and helped them. By midafternoon Anna, Joseph, Brandon, and Madison came to help as well. They placed sheets and blankets on the grass in case people couldn't stand and need to sit. When they were done eating their early supper, they put all the livestock away in their pens and stalls. The late afternoon sky slowly turned into the early evening, the sky was a satin purple, and the stars glittered like heavenly diamonds.

Slowly people started to arrive, from peasants and farmers to noblemen. There were even more people that had come than they expected. Slowly groups of white witches came to hear what they had to say. Just then Ruth made a protective circle around the field, and Ruth and the other white witches placed a cloaking spell all around the group. Then they began the meeting.

"We are all here to discuss the situation we have with Keals," Ruth started to explain. "Keals has done something to Lord Devon. We must work together to put Lord Devon back on the throne."

"What are we supposed to do against Keals and his forces?" one of the farmers asked.

"If we band together as one, we can put a stop to his evil deeds," Ruth called out.

The crowds of people began raising their arms and cheering loudly.

"We will start our preparations morrow," Liza announced.

The crowd slowly dispersed leaving Liza, Isaiah, and Boby alone. They went into the cabin and went to sleep.

In the morning Liza, Ruth, and Boby went to town to make preparations for the rebellion. Liza told her brother Lenn to make an order for swords and not to tell anyone about it. Ruth talked to her friend, the tavern innkeeper, to inform the white witches when and where the rebellion was.

Chapter 9
The Rebellion

A couple of days had passed and the people were preparing for the rebellion. There were groups of people practicing hand-to-hand combat; others were practicing archery and sword fighting. Ruth and the other white witches were going over the spells they were going to be using. Brandon, Madison, and Isaiah were helping with chores; when they were done, they played with Cheats. Sometime later the kids wanted to join in combat training, but their parents wouldn't let them, which sparked an argument. Even though it was cold out, the people were drenched with sweat and were tired. Anna and Liza passed around canteens and they all drank water and rested.

All of a sudden, a royal guard rode up and saw the people combat training. The guard rode back to the castle and reported his findings, not worrying about it Keals went about his business. Keals was getting fed up with how Devon was acting because of his mental digression. Keals grabbed Devon and dragged him to the dungeon, he ordered the guard to open up the dungeon doors. In one of the cells was the councilmember that Keals had arrested at the public assembly.

"I have a friend to keep you company," Keals said as he threw Devon in and locked the cell again.

"Lord Devon, are you okay?" the councilman asked rushing over to Devon. Then he stared at Keals, "You will not get away with this."

"Yeah. Well, we will see about that," Keals said with a smirk.

The day drew on as the afternoon turned into night; the groups of people slowly began to leave. Liza, Scottie, and Ruth got onto the wagon and left, they got to town and made their way to Lenn's shop. Lenn greeted them with hugs and they secretly loaded the swords onto the wagon. They covered the swords with sheets, bid Lenn farewell, and left town. When they got to Ruth's cottage, Ruth went to the stable and opened the secret storage and they placed the swords into it. Liza finally got home an hour later and went to sleep.

The next morning after breakfast, the groups of people returned and continued combat training. Isaiah, Madison, and Brandon talked to their parents about combat training again. Their parents agreed to let them train but only if they promised to only use combat skills in self-defense, so they did. So, they began training at once.

Meanwhile at the castle, Keals was pacing back and forth in the throne room. He had received more complaints about the missing kids and livestock from villagers. Deep inside the gardens, Supay was feasting on children once again. There were torn up bloody carcasses littered all over the grounds of the deepest part of the garden. Keals slowly approached the Black Shadow staring at the Black Shadow with disgust, then he looked down at the carcasses.

"What the hell are you doing? Eating children?" Keals asked in disdain "Feasting on cattle and other livestock is one thing, but you cannot eat children!"

"How dare you talk to me like that, fleshling!" Supay exclaimed.

Just then Supay inhaled deeply, calmed down, and stopped speaking.

"I apologize, I assure you I will not do this again," Supay said.

"You better not eat any more children," Keals said flatly. "But you can have all the livestock you desire."

Keals quickly left the garden because of the strong pungent smell of rotting flesh. Meanwhile in town, Ruth and Scottie were picking up supplies. Ruth and Scottie went to Lenn's shop and he greeted them with hugs. Ruth whispered something into Lenn's ear, and then the three of them talked. A while later Ruth and Scottie left the shop and left town. They slowly made their way to Liza and Boby's farm; when they got there, they found the groups of people already in the middle of combat training. Just then they joined in the training. Minutes weaved into hours as sweat drenched their bodies. It was just before sunset when the groups of people started heading home. Madison, Brandon, and their parents stayed behind to help around the farm. A little while later they left the farm and Isaiah and his parents went to sleep.

The following day they all had their final combat training session. Ruth and the other white witches were making their last spell preparations for the last time. Later that afternoon the final preparations were being made. Joseph, Boby, and the other men began cutting down boulder-sized logs. They secretly and quietly rolled the logs to the forest just outside the castle. All the women tied ropes to the large logs, and the men hoisted the large logs on top of the trees. After resting for a while, they all continued training. The afternoon air went from cold to frigid. It slowly got darker and darker until the sky was a purple satin and the stars twinkled high in the night sky. The group of people began to disperse and went back to their homes.

The following day Liza and Isaiah woke up just before sunrise. Boby was still in a heavy slumber from a drunken stupor from the previous night. With difficulty, Liza and Isaiah woke up Boby and got ready for the day. A while later they hopped on the wagon and rode away. Twenty minutes later they reached Ruth's cottage, Scottie and Ruth helped them load the swords onto the wagon, and Boby covered the swords with a large sheet. Ruth whispered into Liza's ear and the three of them left. When they got back home, they fed the animals and put them back in their pens and stalls.

The sky slowly began turning a dark stormy gray. A couple of hours later the groups of people began to arrive. Moments later Ruth and Scottie arrived; minutes after Madison, Brandon and their parents had come. When everybody had gotten to the field, Ruth gave them a very uplifting speech, while Anna, Liza, and Joseph passed around the swords and crossbows. After the speech, with weapons in hand, they all slowly made their way to the forest. They all reached the forest at the same time. Some of the people climbed into trees as the others hid in bushes and other large shrubbery. The rest of the people assembled in the open.

Keals was in his quarters sitting and thinking about things. All of a sudden, there was a knock at the door, and a guard walked into the room. He informed Keals what was going on outside the castle. They both left the room and Keals went to a balcony in the front of the castle.

"What is the meaning of all of this," Keals asked.

"We are here to fight against your tyranny and to put Lord Devon back on the throne," Ruth called out.

"I am not a tyrant," Keals answered back in a soft calm voice, "and besides, Devon is not well enough to rule on the throne."

"Of course, because you did something to him," Ruth said.

Just then Supay came out onto the balcony.

"How dare you speak like that to someone who is better than you?" Supay yelled.

"No, why do you talk to me, demon," Ruth called out. "Yes, I know you are a demon."

Just then Keals put his hand up.

"If they want a fight, we will give them a fight," Keals said.

Suddenly, both of them left the balcony.

Moments later soldiers and guards poured out of the castle's main entrance led by Keals. Following right behind Keals was Supay. Ruth and Keals stood in front of the two lines of fighters; they both stared into each other's eyes.

"For our freedom and for Old York New. Charge!" Ruth called out.

All of a sudden, lightning ripped through the sky, and claps of thunder filled the dark storm clouded sky.

The two lines of people ran towards each other and they started to fight. Rain started to pour down like a heavy waterfall from the sky. Their drenched clothes made it harder for the villagers to fight. The clanging of swords and blood-curdling screams filled the afternoon air. Keals' guards and soldiers were winning, so the villagers fought even harder.

Two guards plunged their swords into the chest of some villagers; the villagers cried in agony and fell to the ground lifeless. Another guard was about to plunge his sword into Madison's back but Isaiah disarmed the guard with his sword and Brandon slashed the guard in the chest. Madison thanked them both and they parted ways again. Again Keals and his guards and soldiers began to advance.

Ruth and another witch stood back to back casting different spells. All of a sudden, a soldier came and slashed the witch standing behind Ruth. Ruth quickly chanted a spell while aiming it at the guard; he flew off the ground hit a tree and crashed down onto the ground with a loud thud. Ruth picked up the witch and carried her to safety. Just as she laid the witch on the ground, she closed her eyes, and the life slowly extinguished from her body.

"Second line attack!" Ruth yelled loudly.

The villagers that were in the trees and bushes cut the ropes and the boulder-sized logs flew down slamming into guards and soldiers. Spells were being cast in every direction by Ruth and the other witches. Very large bubbles and boils began to gush and ooze all over the bodies of the soldiers and guards that got hit by the spells. Just then a bunch of Black Shadow followers ran onto the battlefield and began fighting.

In each of their hands Anna, Joseph, and Liza held a crossbow and sword. They shot arrows and slashed at a group of Keals' followers. Suddenly someone shot Keals with an arrow, the arrow went through his chest and came out of his back, and blood gushed out of the wound. Guards saw what had happened and dragged him to safety. Supay laid his left hand on the wound and began chanting in demonic tongue, and the wound started to sizzle and close up. Keals jumped up off the ground and ran back onto the battlefield. The guard that helped Keals off the battlefield eyes filled with surprise and his mouth gaped open.

Just then the villagers advanced and began winning again. The Black Shadow saw the change in the battle and became angry. The Black Shadow began a demonic chant and the ground slowly opened up all around them. Slowly from out of the gorge rose winged stone creatures. The creatures had ugly disfigured faces, and they were made of flesh and stone. Their eyes were blazing with fire and their teeth were protruding out of their mouths like sharp jagged daggers. The gargoyle creatures flew in every direction attacking villagers, they slashed at people ripping their limbs off.

All of a sudden, with her dying breath, a villager plunged her sword into Supay's chest. He pulled the sword out and the wound sizzled and closed up. He took the sword and sliced off the villager's head, her head rolled onto the ground and blood gushed out of the severed neck. Supay unhinged his jaw, opened his mouth wide, and swallowed the lady's headless body whole. The gargoyle creatures continued to fly around slashing at the villagers and witches.

Just then Supay began chanting in demonic tongue once again. His body began to distort twisting and warping. Slowly his body morphed into a large mammoth being. The Black Shadow creature was five yards tall with long shaggy hair. Its facial features were distorted and it had huge muscles on every inch of its huge body, and its clothing was shredded up. The creature roared and started thrashing villagers around. One of the people in the trees cut a rope and one of the boulder-sized logs went hurling towards the Black Shadow creature, it caught the log in midair and threw it at a group of villagers. The witches continued to cast spells in all directions and other village continued to fight to no benefit.

Seeing that the tide was changing and the villagers were starting to lose, Boby started running away like a coward. A guard saw him running away and knocked him onto the ground hard. The Black Shadow creature tossed people against boulders and trees like they were balls; it slammed others into the ground decapitating their bodies. The sky became even more threateningly gray and lightning and thunder ripped through the sky. The rain pelted down even harder than before making it even harder for the villagers to fight the battle. There were ripped up carcasses littered all over the battlefield in fresh pools of blood. Hours slowly passed and the battle finally ended, and Keals and his forces were victorious. The huge Black Shadow creature slowly morphed back into Supay.

Only Ruth and two other witches, and a handful of villagers had survived. Just then Keals' guards began gathering the survivors and Keals ordered them to be shackled up. A guard came over to Anna, Joseph, Liza, and Boby and shackled them up. All of a sudden, the kids ran over to their parents.

"Do not worry about us, we will be all right," Liza said to Isaiah. "You are now responsible to keep up the farm."

"But what will become of us?" Brandon asked.

"Do not worry. You children will be taken care of," Anna said.

Just then Ruth ran over to the children and bent down to them in secret.

"Run to the farm and stay there until I arrive," Ruth whispered to them. "And if anyone other than me comes, you four must hide."

"What are you going to do, what if something bad happens to you?" Scottie asked Ruth worryingly "What if you get arrested?"

"Do not worry about me. Now obey me and do as I tell you," Ruth ordered.

They did as they were told and Isaiah, Madison, Brandon, and Scottie ran through the forest without looking back. Forty minutes later, with lungs burning and exhausted, the four of them finally reached the farm. Cheats ran out of the cabin and jumped on Isaiah, knocking him off his feet, and licked him. The children sat on the grass and began petting Cheats, thinking, *Did Keals and his evil forces really win this fight? How could the forces of good and justice loss against evil?* Meanwhile at the castle, the rebellion prisoners were led to the dungeon by Keals and a small group of guards. Anna, Joseph, Liza, Boby, and the others were shoved into cells and the doors were slammed shut behind them.

A guard grabbed Ruth by the neck and dragged her to the throne room. The guard shackled her up to the wall behind the throne and quickly left the room. Keals grabbed Ruth by the hair and pulled her face close to his; he took a deep breath of her neck and smelled it. Then he slowly began caressing her hair.

"I want you to be mine, so you have two choices," Keals began to say. "You can stay here and be my sorceress and my mistress or you can die."

"I will never ever do such a thing!" Ruth roared spitting in Keals' face.

"We will see about that," Keals said grabbing her neck.

He walked over to a table and took off his cloak, armor, and upper garments. He stood there shirtless only wearing leather pants. On the table, there were an assortment of whips and other torture devices. He took the longest whip and walked to the middle of the room. He cracked the whip once and it made a loud sharp whistling sound, and he started whipping Ruth. Twenty minutes later he had stopped and went over to Ruth again. Blood and sweat were trickling down her body, and she was slumped over from exhaustion.

"Have you changed your mind yet?" Keals asked.

Ruth slowly looked up and spat on his face again. He wiped the spit off his face and stared at her with a grin.

"Fortunately for you, I have decided not to kill you after all and to set you free. But, I still have to make an example of you," Keals whispered into her ear. "But do not worry, one day soon I will get you where your heart truly lies."

He walked back to the middle of the room, cracked the whip once again, and continued whipping her. A little while later Keals put the whip back on the table and left the room. Just then two guards unshackled Ruth, grabbed her by the shoulders, and dragged her to the forest near the castle. For a long while, she just laid there totally still. Slowly with searing stinging pain, she gently crawled to a tree. Aided by the tree she carefully got to her feet and slowly left.

It was twilight, a waxing moon was gleaming and the stars were sparkling high above Old York New. Ruth slowly and carefully made her way through the forest; with every step she took, pain stung her whole body from the frigid air hitting her fresh wounds. Two hours later she had reached the farm. She went into the cabin and found Isaiah sleeping at the dining table. She went to the bedrooms and found Scottie sleeping on Isaiah's bed, and Madison and Brandon were sharing Liza and Boby's bed. Relieved that the children were okay she quietly sat by the crackling fire and warmed herself up. Ruth slowly took off her cloak and garments; she threaded a needle and began stitching the open sores and deep gashes and softly chanted. A little while later she dozed off by the fire.

A few hours later the sunshine slowly broke through the window and Ruth woke up uneasily. Even though her wounds had started to heal, her body was still in agony. She looked around calling out but didn't see the children so she slowly went to the window; they were outside feeding the animals in their pens and stalls.

Just then Ruth returned to the chair by the fire, the door opened and Cheats skulked in. He purred and jumped into Ruth's lap and she began to pet him. Moments later she went to the cooking pit, started a fire, and began making breakfast. A while later the children came back in, they all sat at the table, and Scottie stared at Ruth with concern.

"Where were you last night and what did Keals do to you?" Scottie asked.

"Just having some fun with Keals and his guards," Ruth replied trying to laugh the question off.

"Is that what you call the opened wounds and sores you came home with last night?" Scottie asked quietly "Yes, I saw you last night."

"That was nothing," Ruth said.

They all sat there quietly and finished eating their porridge.

The rest of the day went by quietly and sluggishly. That evening they all went out to the field, laid down on the grass, and watched the moon come up. A little while later they went back inside and went to sleep. The following day after they had breakfast, leaving Cheats behind, they all went to town. Everything was unusually normal, although there were even more guards. Ruth and the children went to the magic shop, Ruth purchased some herbs and other things and they quickly left.

They walked through town talking with each other. They discussed how it was very unusual that everything went back to norm only a day after the rebellion. As they were walking they noticed people giving Ruth dirty nasty looks. They went to Lenn's steel shop, and Lenn greeted them all with hugs.

"How are you doing?" Lenn asked Ruth "Are you okay?"

"I am doing fine," Ruth answered, "why do you ask?"

"Little Scottie sent me a message by hawk when he saw you last night," Lenn explained, "I have been worrying about you ever since."

"The real question is, are you okay?" Ruth asked.

"Except for a few bumps I could not be better. They would not do anything too bad to me," Lenn said with a slight laugh. "And besides, they need me. I am the only steelworker for one thousand kilometers."

"Do you know why everything went back to normal so quickly?" Ruth asked.

"Oh, well, you do not know yet? Look at this," Lenn replied handing her a parchment.

A Proclamation from Lord Keals:

All shops and stands in the surrounding area of Old York New MUST be open this day. Those owners whose shops and stands are not opened will be arrested.

"How does he have the audacity to do this?" Ruth exclaimed with anger. "We must be going. We will see you later."

"Would you like me to accompany you five?" Lenn asked.

"No, we will be okay," Ruth replied.

"Okay, just be careful," Lenn said to Ruth. "There is word around town that they blame you for the outcome of the rebellion."

Just then Lenn gave them hugs and bid them farewell.

They left the steel shop and walked around town. They noticed that people were still staring at Ruth. All of a sudden, someone pelted a head of cabbage at Ruth's head. She looked up to see where it came from; a crowd of people was standing there. The crowd stared at Ruth with murder on their faces.

"How dare you show your face around here after the rebellion," a woman shouted.

"What are you talking about?" Ruth asked with anger in her voice.

"Because of you and the rebellion our families are either dead or in prison," a man shouted back.

"All of you knew the consequences of the rebellion before we started it," Ruth replied. She then turned to the children and said, "Let us go. You children should not be around people who are ignorant."

As they were walking away, someone pelted another cabbage at Ruth, ignoring it she kept on walking. They quickly got on the wagon and rode away. For the rest of the day, they spent their time at the farm doing chores and talking.

Chapter 10
Death of a Son and Dipping into Black Witchcraft

The days slowly went by turning into weeks and the air got even more unbearably frigid. Ruth and little Scottie had spent all their time with Isaiah, Madison, and Brandon at the farm. One morning Isaiah woke up at the crack of dawn, got ready, and started doing chores. A little while later Madison came outside.

"Isaiah, we need to talk. Well, you know how each winter your parents have to slaughter a few of your livestock because it gets too much to keep them?" Madison began to say, "Well, it is your responsibility to do this since your parents are not here."

"But I cannot," Isaiah said.

"I understand how you feel, but you must," Madison said softly. "Ruth would have done it, but we all talked and we think you should do it."

Then she handed him a knife.

"If you want, I will be there with you," Madison said.

"No, I think I should do this myself," Isaiah said.

Madison went back into the cabin; Isaiah had decided to slaughter one of the female pigs and her babies. With a heavy heart and knife at hand, Isaiah slowly walked to the pigpen. He led the pig and her babies out of the pen and latched it behind him. He took them to the back of the cabin, knelt down on the ground, and began petting them. He took the knife and slowly slit their throats. Cries and squeals of agony rang through the air as blood oozed out of their throats. Isaiah walked to the stream by the farm, washed the blood off his hands and knife, and went back to the farm. As he went inside, Ruth came out with knives and a bundle of parchment.

Isaiah went straight to his room and laid down on his bed. He didn't want to talk to anyone; he just wanted to be left alone. A little while later he got up and left the room. Ruth was over by the fire pit making lunch; Brandon, Madison, and Scottie were playing with Cheats. Ruth looked up, saw Isaiah, and smiled at him.

"This is what I received from selling the pigs' meat," Ruth said handing him a pouch.

With curiosity, he untied the pouch and opened it; it was a large pile of coins.

"I do not want this," Isaiah answered tying it again and handing it back to her.

Ruth pushed it away. "I am not taking it back, that is yours. Now go wash up, lunch is ready."

Moments later the children set the table and they sat and ate. Ruth ladled up some pig stew, and Isaiah stared at the bowl of stew.

"I am not hungry," Isaiah said, pushing the bowl away. "May I be excused?"

"Yes, you may," Ruth replied.

Isaiah took Cheats and they both went outside.

"Do you think he is all right?" Brandon asked.

"I am not sure. You see my children; he has shed blood for the first time in his life. And when that happens, you lose your true innocence and a piece of yourself," Ruth answered to the question. "We can only wait and see if he will be okay. But I think he will be fine."

The next morning outside Isaiah and Cheats were playing tag with each other. At that moment, they saw someone approaching the farm. The person got closer and closer as they came down the field, it was Lenn. He walked over to Isaiah and hugged him. Cheats growled and tried to scratch at Lenn, Isaiah began petting Cheats and he stopped growling and scratching.

"Do not worry, this is Lenn papa. Say hello to him," Isaiah said.

Cheats leaped into Lenn's arms and began licking his face.

"Let us go and talk inside," Lenn said.

When they got inside, Lenn put Cheats down and Ruth smiled at Lenn.

"Come, kids, let us give them time to talk," Ruth said.

Then they went outside and Lenn and Isaiah began talking.

"How are you children doing?" Lenn asked.

"We are okay I guess," Isaiah replied.

"Did you see how your parents are doing?" Lenn asked.

"How can we? The castle is more secure than King Tut's treasure. If we try to go there, we will be arrested for sure, or even worse," Isaiah said.

"There is a secret entrance that Lord Devon used to make me use when he placed the orders for the swords." Lenn began to say, "I can show you the way if you swear only to use it with Ruth's permission."

"Okay, I promise," Isaiah said.

Lenn took a piece of parchment and an inked feather and began making a map. Then Lenn showed Isaiah the map and told him detailed instructions of the way. Isaiah rolled up the map and put it in his room, and then he and Lenn sat by the fire and continued to talk. A few minutes later Ruth and the kids came back inside and they joined the conversation, as they talked Lenn and Ruth smiled at each other lovingly. Moments later Lenn got up, bid them farewell, and he left the farm. The afternoon sluggishly went on turning into evening. While Isaiah was outside putting the farm animals away, Ruth and the others ate the leftover pig stew for supper. When Isaiah came back inside, they all went to sleep.

In the morning Isaiah woke up and looked around, Ruth and little Scottie were still sleeping. He quietly crept to his parent's room and woke up Madison and Brandon; they both yawned and rubbed the sleep out of their eyes.

"I am sorry for waking you up but I am going to the castle to see my parents," Isaiah started to say. "Would you like to come with me?"

"We cannot. If we go, we will surely be arrested," Brandon said.

"No, we will not. My uncle knows of a secret passage, and he has given me a map," Isaiah said.

"But we could still get arrested," Madison said.

"No, we will not, because I have a plan," Isaiah said very softly. "Now are you coming or not? Because I am going."

"Okay, let us just tell Ruth that we are going as well," Brandon said.

"No, Ruth does not know. If we tell her, she will try to stop us," Isaiah said.

Isaiah shoved three sacks into his pocket and put a small knife into his belt. He grabbed three walking staffs and gave one to each Brandon and Madison and they left the room. They quickly and quietly left the cabin and went to the stable, Isaiah petted the horses to calm them down. He took the reins of both horses and slowly walked them out of the stable. With some difficulty, Brandon and Madison pulled the wagon behind them. When they got to the field, Isaiah hitched the wagon to the horses, the three of them hopped on and rode away.

They reached town just before sunrise and tied up the horses. The place was so empty that it looked like a ghost town. Isaiah took the sacks out of his pocket and the knife out of his belt. He cut three holes in each sack and placed the knife back into his belt. Isaiah handed Madison and Brandon each a sack and they put them over their faces, the sack resembled masks. Then they quickly made their way to the forest just outside the castle.

They hid behind trees and cheeked to see if the coast was clear of the guards. They snuck into the clearing and ran over to a huge overgrown oak tree that the map indicated. Isaiah began knocking on the trunk of the tree; all of a sudden, he found a hollowed section of the Oak. He lifted and removed a piece of bark and he, Brandon, and Madison crawled into the oak tree. The inside of the oak tree was so spacious that it could have fit about eight people. There was a narrow path in the Oak so they followed it; the path led deeper and deeper underground, and it led into a simple sewage system. Isaiah took out the map, looked at it, and slipped it back into his pocket. They got into the sewage water and followed it as the map indicated. A little while later they had reached a storm drain, they pulled off the storm drain grates with difficulty and climbed through.

They followed another narrow path until they reached the open space of the dungeon. Just then they started looking for their parents. All the rebellion prisoners had bags under their eyes from their sleepless nights, the men's facial hair was becoming shaggy and untamed. Minutes later Isaiah found his parents. He took the sack off his face and Liza gawked at him.

"I found them," Isaiah called out.

Just then Madison and Brandon came over.

"What are you children doing here?" Anna asked.

"We wanted to see you so we came," Brandon answered.

"How did you find us?" Liza asked.

"Well, Lenn papa knows of a secret passageway and he gave me a map of it," Isaiah replied.

"We are very glad to see you. But you must go now before you children are caught," Anna said.

Not even a second after those words were uttered, they heard shouting and footsteps storming down the stairs. The three of them quickly placed the sacks on their heads once again and held onto their walking staffs tightly ready to fight. Just then a group of guards came storming through the prison entrance.

"Intruders! Get them!" a guard yelled.

The guards ran towards Brandon, Madison, and Isaiah and started battling. They bashed the guards in the face with the ends of their walking staffs. Isaiah jumped into the air and kicked two guards in the face. Madison double head-butted two guards. The guards fell to the ground face down, the children smiled at their parents and ran the way they came from. They covered their tracks as best as they could. A little while later they climbed out of the giant oak tree and ran through the forest.

When they reached the forest clearing, they took the sacks off their heads. With burning lungs and out of breath Isaiah put the sacks back into his pocket and the three of them slowly walked into town. They went to Lenn's shop and told him about what happened;

Isaiah took the map out of his pocket and gave it back to Lenn. They bid Lenn farewell and left the shop. They slowly made their way to the wagon. Isaiah untied the horses; the children hopped on the wagon and rode away.

When they got back to the farm, Ruth was waiting for them in the opened doorway; she had anger in her face. Isaiah put the horses back into the stable and the children walked to the cabin together. When they got to the door, they looked at Ruth and looked down to the ground, they knew they were in big trouble.

"Before you come in will you tell me where you were," Ruth said as the temper in her voice rose.

"We went to the castle to see our parents," Madison replied.

"How did you go there and get back without getting caught?" Ruth asked trying to remain calm.

"Uncle Lenn gave me a map for a secret passage so we followed it. And we also had these," Isaiah replied showing her the sack masks.

"How dare you go without telling me? You did not even leave me a note," Ruth yelled, her anger boiling over. "Now go do the chores."

Just then the children went and fed the farm animals and cleaned out their stalls and pens. When they were done with the chores, they went to the stream by the cabin and washed up. They slowly went back to the cabin and found lunch waiting for them on the table. They sat down at the table and ate quietly; they had meat and potatoes for lunch. The cabin was silent since Ruth and Scottie left. The dishes were washed, dried, and put away. After that they sat around and talked, Cheats jumped onto Isaiah's lap and he started petting Cheats.

The afternoon drew on slowly turning into evening. Just before sunset, they heard a popping sound just outside and Ruth and Scottie came inside and went straight to Liza and Boby's room. Moments later Ruth came over and glared at them.

"You were not only dishonest with me but you were dishonest with Lenn as well," Ruth said frowning and shaking her head.

She went over to the fireplace and sat down near the crackling fire. Just then Scottie motioned to them from the doorway of Isaiah's room. The children went into the room and Isaiah closed the door behind himself.

"I did not realize that your mother was this mad at us," Isaiah said.

"Mother is not mad at you guys. She is just very disappointed," Scottie began to explain. "But do not worry, she will forgive you in time."

The children stayed up for a little while longer and they retired for the night. Early the following morning they all woke up and the children began doing chores. After their breakfast of porridge and fruit, Ruth gathered Isaiah, Madison, and Brandon by the dining table.

"I just wanted to tell you three that I am still disappointed and upset with you. But even though I am upset with you, I should have not went off on you like that," Ruth said to the three of them. "Now go get ready. We must go to Anna and Joseph's cottage to check on things."

The three of them got up and went to the bedroom, and Isaiah stopped at the doorway.

"I am sorry as well," he said.

Moments later, the children came out of the bedroom and left the cabin. They hitched the wagon to the horses and rode away. They stopped by Ruth's cottage and she grabbed two spellbooks and a small pouch of herbs. She unhitched the horses and tied them up in the back. It was unusually warm for a winters' day. Ruth told the children that it would be nice and enjoyable to walk to the cottage so they did. As they were walking, there was a loud crackling and crunching of leaves and twigs, Ruth stopped and looked around, not seeing anyone or anything they continued walking.

When they got to the cottage, Madison and Brandon ran inside, inhaling the sweet smells of their home. The others came inside and Ruth put her things on the dining table. Just then Ruth and the children began cleaning up the cottage. A little while later Ruth grabbed her spellbooks and went outside, a light breeze blew through the air. The breeze blew onto Ruth's face, she closed her eyes and thought of her long-deceased husband. She sat under a tree and began reading her spellbooks.

All of a sudden, she looked up and saw two people coming down the field. As they approached Ruth realized it was Keals and Supay. Keals grinned at Ruth and pulled out a crossbow and as he was loading it, he lit the arrowhead with fire and shot it. The arrow pierced the cottage and the flames slowly began spreading, just then Keals shot more flaming arrows at the cottage. The children smelled the smoke and ran out of the house. Keals saw Scottie and ran over to him; he grabbed Scottie and pulled a dagger to him.

"I told you that I would get you where your heart truly lies," Keals called out.

He stabbed Scottie twice in the stomach twisting the dagger around.

"NOOO, little Scottie!" Ruth yelled.

Supay grabbed Keals and they both quickly disappeared.

Ruth ran over to Scottie and held him tightly. Scottie smiled widely as blood slowly trickled down out of the wound. The light from his eyes slowly faded and he laid there lifeless. Her son was dead, killed senselessly. Ruth threw herself over little Scottie and wept bitterly. The flames slowly spread over the cottage and the fire engulfed the whole house.

She felt a rage that could only be calmed by revenge. Ruth got up and opened up her spell book of black witchcraft. She stared at the pages of the book and began speaking in strange tongue; the words faded off the pages and appeared on Ruth's face.

The sky turned a dark grey and thunder, and lightning ripped through the sky. Ruth quickly teleported herself to the castle with revenge building up in her heart.

Meanwhile at the castle, Keals was talking with Supay in the throne room. Just then there was a popping sound and Ruth appeared in midair. She came down and jabbed Keals in the face with her walking staff. Supay chanted and Ruth flew into a wall and fell to the ground. She slowly got up and began chanting aloud; the Black Shadow flew into the air and shot out of the room, and the doors slammed shut. Ruth began chanting in strange tongue once again, and deep gashes slashed across Keals' face.

All of a sudden, the door blew open and the Black Shadow ran back into the room. Supay grabbed Ruth and threw her across the room. Ruth's eyes turned pitch black and she began to chant again. The flames of the candles around the room blew out and more deep gashes slashed across the Black Shadow's face.

Ruth jumped into the air and jabbed at the Black Shadow with her walking staff. She tried to jab him again when Supay grabbed the walking staff and threw her across the room again, she hit a wall and fell to the ground with a loud thud. The demon glided over to Ruth, grabbed her by the neck, and continuously slammed her into a wall. Supay grabbed Ruth and they teleported away. Meanwhile at Joseph and Anna's home, the cottage was in shambles, everything was destroyed. Scottie's lifeless body laid by a tree. The children stared at the charred rubble that was the remains of the cottage.

Right then Supay and Ruth popped out of thin air, dropped Ruth on the ground, and Supay disappeared again. The children saw Ruth laying there totally still, so Isaiah ran to Ruth's house. He hitched the horses, jumped on the wagon, and rode away as fast as possible. When he got back to the others, they placed little Scottie's lifeless body onto the wagon and covered it with a sheet. Then they placed Ruth onto the wagon with difficulty, Isaiah grabbed the spellbooks, the children climbed on and rode away.

When they got to the farm, they carried and laid Ruth on Liza's bed. Madison opened the white witchcraft book and looked through it, moments later she found a healing incantation. She began mixing herbs into a bowl turning it into a paste. Just then Madison began chanting the healing spell. Isaiah wrote a message, tied it to a messenger hawk's talon, and it flew outside. A half-hour later the hawk came back, Isaiah tied another rolled up piece of parchment to its talons, and it flew away again.

When Madison was done with the spell, the three of them sat around and talked. Time passed by and minutes turned into hours. Around midnight Ruth slowly began stirring, a little while later she yawned loudly and with pain wiped the sleep out of her eyes. She asked the children where Scottie's body was and she went out to the wagon and wept over the body.

The following morning Ruth and the kids woke up and got ready. Moments later there was a knock at the door so Ruth answered it, it was Lenn. He came inside and Ruth broke down crying in his arms. Just then the door opened and a monk came inside. He gave them his condolences and began blessing them. Then they all went outside and the monk blessed Scottie's body as they prayed.

"It is time," the monk said.

Lenn picked Scottie up and followed behind Ruth, the monk, and the children in a solemn line. Moments later they reached a small family burial plot where Ruth's husband and other family members were laid to rest. Lenn laid Scottie on the ice-cold ground and began digging a hole. When Lenn was finished digging, the monk blessed Scottie's body and the ground with holy water and wrapped the body with sheets and bandages. They began singing sad hymns and wept bitter mourning. Moments later Lenn and the monk placed Scottie's body in the hole, the monk sprinkled holy water on the body and the ground again, and Lenn covered the body with dirt. When he was done, they slowly departed.

The monk left and they went back to Ruth's cottage. Lenn stayed for a little while longer and then left. Ruth quietly did chores, trying to just keep herself busy in her time of grief.

Meanwhile at the castle, Keals and the Black Shadows were sitting around talking.

"Everything is going according to plan," Supay said.

"What are your plans?" Keals asked.

"You do not have to know about our plans just yet," Supay answered.

"Yes, but I feel I should know these plans," Keals said.

"I will let you know our plans when the time is right," Supay said.

Chapter 11
The Warrior of Raw

Slowly the hours turned into days, and the days wove into weeks. Everything was still quite gloomy from the death of little Scottie, Ruth slowly started her daily routines once again. One morning after breakfast, Ruth gathered the children around the dining table, and they talked and remembered the good times with little Scottie. A little while later Ruth told the children to get ready to go into town. Moments later the kids went outside and waited for Ruth. Just then she came outside and locked the door behind herself. Ruth hitched the wagon to the horses, and they got on and rode away.

When they got to town, Isaiah tied up the horses and they walked around town. Around midafternoon, after having lunch at the tavern, they went to Lenn's shop. Lenn greeted them with hugs and took Ruth aside. They both began talking softly and whispering to each other, the kids tried to hear what they were saying but couldn't. Moments later they came back to where the kids were and they all started talking. The five of them went into the metal works shop. In the right-hand corner of the shop was a long workbench, and there was something on it covered by a sheet. Lenn saw that they were looking and told them that he was working on a secret project. A while later Lenn bid them farewell and they left.

Sometime later they left town and went to the farm. Isaiah went into the cabin, got Cheats, and went to the wagon again. When they got to Ruth's cottage, the kids went inside, sat by the crackling fire, and started playing with Cheats. When Ruth came inside, she started preparing supper, and the children set the table. When the food was ready, they said grace and started eating. After dinner Ruth did a spell to make the cottage roof invisible, and they watched as the sun set and the moon rose. Later they went to sleep.

The following morning, they woke up late, Ruth went over to the window and inhaled the fresh air. The sky was filled with dark gray storm clouds; it looked as though it would rain at any time. Just then she started doing chores and the kids helped her. After their breakfast of porridge, Ruth went to the stream near her cottage and began washing the dishes and the kids dried them and put them away. Later Ruth gathered the children around the dining table.

"Isaiah, I must talk to you and tell you something. Your mother was going to tell you this after the rebellion," Ruth began to say to Isaiah. "I wanted your Uncle Lenn to tell you, but he said I should be the one to tell you. This knowledge might help in the fight against the Black Shadows."

Just then she began telling a tale.

Sometime after Christ was crucified, the apostle Paul had a great weapon against evil in his possession called, the Eye of God. The Eye of God was a torch, and when lit, had the power to cast demons that had possessed a person back to Hell. Before his death, Paul gathered a small group of monks; the group consisted of five young monks including your mother's grandfather Mathais.

Isaiah had a surprised look on his face as the kids listened intently.

Paul requested for the monks to go on a quest to hide this great weapon. For some time, the monks trained in the art of battle, but still kept their monk ways in their minds and hearts. Sometime later their training ended and they started their mission to hide the Eye of God. With many difficulties and numerous obstacles trying to stop them, they managed to hide the great weapon. Eventually Mathais fell in love, and with much prayer got wedded.

"What was the name of this secret group and what happened to them," Isaiah asked.

"The group's name was the Warriors of Raw. And after the wedding, Mathais' wife joined the group," Ruth explained, answering the question. "Eventually the group broke apart going their separate ways."

"I wish we knew more about the Warriors of Raw," Isaiah commented.

"Well, you can. But it will have to wait until morrow," Ruth said.

For the rest of the day, the children talked about the story as they did chores. Hours slowly passed and Ruth fell asleep. It was around midnight when the kids fell asleep. Early the next morning, Ruth woke the kids up and they began the chores; after breakfast, they got on the wagon and rode away. A little while later they reached the farm. They tied the horses up and found Lenn waiting for them. Lenn led them to their family burial plot.

When they got to the outer edge of the burial plot, Lenn went to the center and walked seven paces into the burial plot and he began to dig. The boys grabbed spades and helped Lenn to dig. Moments later they hit something solid, they scraped at the dirt until they exposed one entire side of a box-like object. Isaiah ran his fingers over it. It felt to be twelve inches in height and eighteen inches wide. He had no idea how far into the earth it extended. He tried pulling it out but it wouldn't budge. They dug all around the solid object to reveal a wooden crate. They slowly lifted the crate out of the hole with difficulty and placed it onto the ground. They carefully wiped the caked-on dirt off the crate. The wooden crate was ancient looking and it had a heavy lock on it. They picked up the crate and carried it back to the farm.

When they got back to the farm, they put the crate gently on the ground. Thinking it would be much easier to break Isaiah pulled at the lock but it wouldn't budge. Lenn took his spade and smashed the lock, there was a click and the lock broke. Lenn moved aside but Isaiah asked "why." Lenn replied that he had to do this himself. Isaiah lifted the crate open to reveal two bundles wrapped in cloth; covered in dust and cobwebs. He brushed the dust off them and took the bundles out. Lenn told Madison and Brandon to give Isaiah some time alone. Isaiah then went to his room, closed the door, and put the bundles on the floor. He sat on his bed and stared at the bundles for a long while. A while later he knelt on the floor and unwrapped the bundles.

In the first bundle, there was an old worn-out leather-bound notebook. In the center of the cover was a symbol. The symbol was the crucifix in the middle of the sun, and there were two angel wings on the right and left sides of the sun. It was encircled in a circle. Then he unwrapped the second bundle to reveal slightly rusted warrior armor. The armor was simple and crude; made of strips of metal that were woven together. The same symbol that was on the notebook was on the center of the armor as well. Isaiah ran his fingers over the armor and notebook, and stared at them for a while.

A little while later, he opened his bedroom door and told them they could come in. He showed them the things that were in the old wooden crate. Lenn told them that the symbol was the crest of the Warriors of Raw. They left the bedroom; they sat at the dining table and talked.

"What are you going to do with these things?" Isaiah asked.

"I will not be doing anything with them. This is your journey to take," Lenn said to Isaiah. "I trust you will do the right thing."

"Let us give him some time alone," Ruth said and she turned to Brandon and Madison. "You two will be staying with me for now. Now please, let us leave."

Eventually, the three of them left.

"I am going to leave as well. I will come over again soon to see how you are doing," Lenn said.

They both hugged each other and Lenn departed, leaving Isaiah alone contemplating the events that unfolded.

When Isaiah finished feeding the farm animals and cleaning out their pens and stalls, he played with Cheats. That evening after the chores, Isaiah made a small pot of beef stew; he sat down and ate. He fed the leftovers to Cheats and washed the dishes. Isaiah went and sat by the crackling fire; Cheats leaped on his lap and eventually fell asleep. Moments later, Isaiah gently put Cheats on the floor and went to his room. He grabbed the old notebook and went back to where he was sitting. As soon as he opened the book, he saw a name written there:

Chacko Mathais

He turned two more pages and saw the first journal entry.

Paul the apostle requested me to lead a small group of my fellow monks on a special mission to hide the Eye of God. The Eye of God is a very important and holy weapon against the forces of evil. But before we go on this journey Paul informed us that we will have to go through battle training. I fear what the training will do to our souls but with much prayer we will be okay.

We have just completed our first training session in hand-to-hand combat and I do not feel different. With a lot of prayer and reflection of our hearts and souls, we will be okay. We will be doing training with weapons soon.

The entry ended so he turned to the next page.

I have not written in this journal for a while, we have been working hard on hand-to-hand combat. The day after next, we will begin weapons training. This will be the very first time ever that I, or any of the other monks, will wield any sort of weapon. Just thinking about it makes me feel uneasy, but I am sure we will be fine. We monks have finally witnessed the power of the Eye of God. I am not sure how it works but when the torch is lit with a flame, it sucks out the evil spirit or demon from the possessed body and casts it back to hell.

As he was reading, Isaiah fell asleep on the chair.

The following morning Isaiah woke up, the ash embers was the only thing left from the fire, and Cheats was still sleeping by his feet. After eating his breakfast of porridge, Isaiah began doing farm chores. Later that afternoon, Madison and Brandon came over to hangout. Isaiah told them that the book was the journal of his great grandfather Chacko Mathais. That afternoon the children took Cheats outside and played with him. It slowly got darker and darker and Brandon and Madison went back to Ruth's cottage. Both Isaiah and Cheats sat by the fireplace warmed by the crackling fire and Isaiah began thinking. He grabbed the journal and began reading.

We have completed our final training and we will be beginning our journey in one day's time. We are trying to relax until then but it is hard knowing the challenges we are about to face. We were told by Paul that there will be a lot of obstacles and forces trying to stop us on the journey. I am going to go pray and meditate for a while before we have supper.

He continued to read but nothing interesting happened until he got to the middle of the journal.

It is the fifth day of our journey and we have witnessed the power of some demons. A demon had possessed one of the monks that have come with us on the journey. I lit the Eye of God and repeated the words that Paul told me to say; as soon as I did, the demon was cast out of the monk and sent back to hell. With much prayer and meditation, we will get through this safety.

Isaiah went to his bedroom, put away the journal, and went to sleep.

In the morning Cheats slowly crept into the room and Isaiah woke up startled. He yawned loudly and began his day. After the chores and breakfast, he played with Cheats. A little while later they both went to the stream, as Isaiah bathed Cheats splashed around in the water. When they got back to the farm, Isaiah hung his wet clothes on the line and put on some dry clothes. The day quickly drew on and he ended the evening chores by cleaning the pens and stalls of the animals. When he was done eating dinner, he took the journal, sat by the fireplace, and started reading.

We have only one more day of traveling until we reach the place we will be hiding the Eye of God. But before that, we must stop at the house of a sorceress. Paul said that this sorceress has helped him many times before and she will help us hide the Eye of God. Paul informed me that she is a sorceress of White Witchcraft and her name is Aley.

We have spoken to Aley and she has agreed to come and help us. Aley is from India, the same land that I have come from. She is quite a fetching young maiden, but she is two ages younger than I am. I feel bad that I am feeling this way.

He continued reading and a little while later he reached the last page of the journal entries.

We have finally reached the cavern that we will be hiding the Eye of God in. Aley has placed a protection enchantment around the cavern. I have made a map for the time to come for those who need the Eye of God to fight the forces of Evil. God bless you and may peace be with you always.

He turned the page and a loose folded piece of parchment fell out. Isaiah picked it up and unfolded it; it was the map. He looked at the map over and over again. Moments later he put the map away and went to sleep.

The following day Isaiah woke up, washed up, and got ready for the day. After the morning chores, he went inside; grabbed an inked feather and a piece of parchment, and began writing. He tied the parchment to the hawk's talons and it flew away.

He went to his bedroom and laid on his bed. As he lay there, he thought about the events of the past couple of days. *How did Paul obtain the Eye of God? And did Paul and his Great Grandfather really want the Eye of God to be found and used again?* All these questions swirled through his head as the morning slowly turned into noon. After eating lunch he grabbed Cheats, hitched the wagon to the horses, and rode away.

A little while later he reached Ruth's cottage, tied the horses up, and knocked on the door. Moments later the door opened and Madison stood smiling at him. Isaiah hugged her and he went inside and closed the door behind himself. There was another knock at the door, and Ruth answered it, it was Lenn.

"How are you doing? Is everything okay?" Ruth asked.

"Yes, everything is just fine. Isaiah sent me a message that said to come here," Lenn replied as he closed the door.

Then they all sat at the dining table and began talking.

"I have thought a lot these past few days, and I have a question," Isaiah said to Lenn. "Did you know what was in the crate before we dug it up?"

"Well, your mother and I knew the items in the crate belonged to the Warriors of Raw but we did not know exactly what," Lenn started to explain. "Through the years our family has pledged to keep this a secret until the day that the world needs the Warriors of Raw once again. And I think this is the time."

"Are you saying that we should bring back the group the Warriors of Raw?" Isaiah asked.

"That must be your choice," Lenn answered.

"Then I think we should resurrect the Warriors of Raw," Isaiah said.

"Are you sure that this is a wise decision?" Ruth asked.

"If we resurrect the Warriors of Raw, it might give us an edge to defeat the Black Shadow. Either way, we must retrieve the Eye of God to defeat the Black Shadow," Isaiah responded.

"If you really want to resurrect the Warriors of Raw, you will need a lot of training," Lenn said.

"Who will be in the group with you?" Ruth asked.

"We will," Brandon and Madison answered.

"I cannot ask you two to risk your lives and well-being," Isaiah said.

"Look, you need people you can trust when you put the Warriors of Raw back together," Brandon said to Isaiah. "And we have known each other since birth, you are like our brother."

"What he is saying is true and you know it," Madison said.

"Doing this will be risky," Isaiah announced.

"We are prepared for all the risks," Brandon said.

"Okay, fine," Isaiah said.

"If you are serious about this, we must begin training right away," Ruth said.

"Okay, whatever we need to do," Isaiah said.

"And are you two ready for what needs to be done?" Ruth asked Brandon and Madison.

"Yes, we are," they both answered.

"Okay, then get your walking staffs and meet me outside," Ruth told the kids.

Isaiah, Madison, and Brandon grabbed their walking staffs and they went outside and waited for Ruth. Moments later Ruth and Lenn came outside with their walking staffs at hand. They stood in fighting stance and began attacking the kids. They trained in combat for so long that their bodies and clothes were drenched in sweat and they were bruised up and in pain. After they ate lunch, they continued their battle training. As soon as the sun went down Lenn bid them farewell and left the cottage. After they watched the moon rise, Ruth and the kids went inside and went to sleep.

Ruth woke up the kids early the following morning. They had scrambled eggs, roasted meat, and mugs of milk for breakfast and then started battle training. A little while later Lenn came over and helped Ruth with the training session. Throughout the day the loud thuds of the wooden walking staffs banging against each other echoed through the air. Sometime later they rested and drank their afternoon tea, and after they continued their training.

All of a sudden, a castle guard appeared on horseback. He saw from the distance Ruth, Lenn, and the kids in the middle of their battle training. He quickly rode back to the castle and reported what he had seen to Keals and the Black Shadows. They weren't worried about what they heard, so they told the guard to leave the room.

Meanwhile at the cabin, they ended the training and were having supper. After dinner, Ruth left the farm. Minutes later she reached Lenn's house, and she and Lenn began talking. Sometime later she left and went back to the farm. The kids went to the bedrooms and went to sleep; Ruth sat by the crackling fire and stared into the flames. She was thinking of her poor son and all he was missing.

The following morning Isaiah woke up at the crack of dawn and started doing chores. A while later Ruth called him in for breakfast, he washed up at the stream and went inside. When they were done eating, they began their battle training. Later that afternoon Lenn rode up on a wagon, he stopped in front of the cabin and got off. In the back of the wagon, there was a pile of thin strips of scrap metal and steel.

"Hi Lenn papa, what is that scrap metal and steel for?" Isaiah asked.

"We will be making your armor today. And we will be using this," Lenn answered.

Lenn and the boys pulled the wagon to the workbench at the back of the cabin. They put the scrap metal on the workbench and the kids started making their armor. They wove the strips of metal and steel tightly together. Lenn took some of the strap metal, melted it down, and began making the Warriors of Raw symbols. When the symbols were cooled and ready, the kids took them and secured them to the armor's chest plates. A while later they were finished making the armor, so the kids put the armor on and began battle training. That evening, Lenn left and Ruth and the kids went to sleep.

The following day there was a loud screeching just outside the cabin. All of a sudden, a messenger hawk flew through the window. Isaiah took the parchment off the talon of the hawk and read it aloud. After lunch,

Ruth and the kids began training. As the day went on their bodies and clothes were drenched in sweat. A while later they washed up in the stream and Ruth made a list of the things she needed from town. Moments later they got onto the wagon and rode into town. When they got there, Isaiah tied the horses up and they went shopping for the provisions. The last shop they went to was the magic shop.

It slowly became darker and darker and nightfall finally arrived. The town was dark and quiet except for three stands that were open. Ruth and the children slowly made their way to Lenn's shop. They entered the shop but nobody was there. Moments later Lenn had come back to the shop and greeted them with hugs.

"Hi Lenn papa, you wanted to see us?" Isaiah asked.

"You kids will be making your weapons tonight," Lenn said to the children. "But we will have to wait until the town is totally empty."

Sometime later the very last stand owner said goodnight to Lenn and left town. Just then Lenn grabbed large piles of scrap steel and started melting it down, and poured the molten steel into sword casts. When the metal and steel was cool enough, the kids began banging out the metal and steel into swords and thinking: BANG! *Could finding the Eye of God really help in the fight against the Black Shadows?* BANG! *Could reforming the Warriors of Raw help in the fight as well?* BANG!

When they were finished making the swords, they set them aside and Lenn poured some molten metal and steel out again. When it was ready to work with, the children started forging the metal into shields. When the swords and shields were ready, they loaded them onto the back of the wagon on top of a pile of straw, and they put more straw on top. Then they bid Lenn farewell, and Ruth and the children got on the wagon and they left town.

For the next couple of days, the children did battle training wearing their new armor and using their new shields. Late one afternoon a messenger hawk came to the farm and flew onto Isaiah's right shoulder. Isaiah untied a rolled-up piece of parchment and read it aloud. After, they continued the battle training. Later that evening after doing chores and eating supper they got onto the wagon and rode away. A while later they got to town just as the shops and stands were closing for the night.

Isaiah tied the horses up and they went to Lenn's shop. When they got there, nobody was there, not ever Lenn. Seconds later there was a knock at the door and Lenn came inside. He smiled and greeted them with hugs.

"How are you doing?" Lenn asked.

"We are just fine. You wanted to see us?" Ruth answered.

"Yes, I finished that secret project I was working on, and I wanted to show it to you," Lenn began explaining to them. "This might help you in the fight."

They went over to the workbench and Lenn pulled off the sheet. The object was compact and made entirely of metal. It had a long shaft and a barrel and a short handle, and it had a trigger mechanism on it. Next to the object were three small metal balls.

"What is that thing?" Isaiah asked.

"I call it a *Pistol*," Lenn answered.

"How does it work?" Madison asked.

"Well, you put this powder into the barrel. Place the metal ball in with this plug and pull the trigger," Lenn began to explain. "The ball will shoot out at a high speed at the target that you are aiming at."

"So, it is basically a mini cannon," Isaiah said.

"Yes, yes it is," Lenn said.

At that second, he grabbed a stuffed sack and they went outside, he tied the sack to the side of the shop. Then he showed them how to use it. A while later Ruth and the kids left town and went back to Ruth's cottage.

Chapter 12

The Evil Plans of the Black Shadow

The brutal and bitter cold of winter slowly died down and the gentle cooling warmth of spring finally arrived. It was a beautiful morning and Ruth and the children woke up early to begin their battle training. Meanwhile at the castle, things were quiet. Everywhere that you could go in the castle, you could see pools of blood and carcasses all over. Everyone in the castle except for Keals was in fear for their lives because of the actions and activities of the Black Shadow. Keals and the Black Shadow were discussing matters in the throne room.

Moments later Keals and the Black Shadow left the throne room and the Black Shadow made its way to the royal graveyard. There were pools of blood all over and there were dismembered carcasses littered all over the catacombs. The Black Shadow walked over to a large pool of blood and started chanting. All of a sudden, the pool of blood started bubbling and boiling over.

Just then a dark and demonic image appeared in the pool of blood. The demon had long brown hair and black yellow eyes, and the demon looked female. Flames danced all around the demoness as its eyes started glowing brightly.

"How are our plans coming along?" the demoness asked.

"They're coming along nicely Queen Lilith," Supay started to say. "We have enough followers to do the ceremony. We just have to wait for the next blood moon."

The demoness' eyes began glowing again and the demons began laughing. Two guards brought a group of shackled up people to them and the guards left again. The demons glared at the people and began drooling and snarling at them, and the people started crying and screaming for help. Lilith pressed her long bony fingers against an invisible barrier. Just then the pool of blood started to sizzle and the barrier burned Lilith.

"I'm sorry your highness but the barrier still holds strong," Supay said.

"Not to worry, soon the barrier will be weak and unstable and I will be able to escape," Lilith said.

Slowly Lilith's image faded away and the Black Shadow started to snarl and howl in hunger. Just then blood splattered everywhere.

Chapter 13
Unexpected Help

The following morning everybody on the farm woke up early and got ready for the day. By midafternoon Ruth and the kids were deep in battle training. After training and having lunch, Ruth left the farm leaving the children alone. When she got to her cottage, Ruth grabbed her white witchcraft books and other books and began reading them. Just before sundown she put the books in the wagon and left the cottage. When she got back to the farm, she tied the horses up in the stable and took the books inside. The kids had dinner waiting for her so they all sat down to eat. After dinner, the kids went to sleep early and Ruth stayed up to read.

The following day after breakfast, Lenn came over and the kids began their training. That afternoon they had a very light lunch, and after they continued the training while Ruth once again read her books. The gentle spring breeze cooled off the sweat-drenched bodies of the children and Lenn. Later that afternoon they washed up in the stream and the kids started the farm chores and Lenn helped them.

After dinner, Ruth gathered the children and Lenn around the dining table.

"To find the Eye of God and succeed in the battle against the Black Shadow we must get help, unconventional help." Ruth started explaining to them, "We will be calling on the assistance of the creatures known as Centaurs."

"I thought magical creatures such as that did not really exist," Isaiah commented.

"Well, magical creatures such as centaurs and other beings exist in an alternate parallel world known as the Moundewdun world," replied Ruth.

"What is an alternate parallel world?" Lenn asked.

"It is a world just like ours that exists in a different realm. In this Moundewdun world, all magical beings exist," Ruth continued explaining to them. "In that world, magic is everywhere and in everything."

"How are you going to ask for their help if they are in this parallel world?" Lenn asked.

"Well, we must use spells and incantations. I will explain to you in full morrow."

They continued talking for a while longer and around twilight Lenn left.

The next day Ruth saw someone on a wagon approaching from the distance. As the person got closer and closer she realized it was one of the shopkeepers with the provisions for the farm. She told the children to go inside and stay in the bedroom until the shopkeeper leaves so they did as they were told. Right after he unloaded the provisions, the shopkeeper left. When he was well away from the farm borders and from viewing sight, Ruth whistled and the kids came back outside and continued training. That evening after dinner, Lenn came over and they began preparing everything.

A little while later the brightly lit moon was high above Old York New. Ruth started gathering all the magical herbal ingredients she needed for working the incantations and spells she was about to perform. She sat down Lenn and the kids and explained everything to them.

"We will be performing some powerful sorcery. We will be opening the Temporal-Lobe of Anubus. Only by doing this can we call upon the Moundewdun world," Ruth explained.

"What is this Temporal-Lobe of Anubus?" Isaiah asked.

"It is an invisible gateway barrier between both our realms," Ruth began explaining. "And it could only be opened by magical sources."

"So, we will be opening this Temporal-Lobe of Anubus now?" Brandon asked.

"No, tonight we will only have some small access to the Temporal-Lobe of Anubus," Ruth answered.

"How can centaurs help us defeat demons?" Madison asked.

"We will not be calling just any ordinary centaurs. We will be asking for help from Elemental Centaurs. These centaurs weald the powers of the four elements," Ruth explained.

Ruth took out a large round shallow bowl and filled it with water. She then opened one of her spellbooks, put magical herbs into the bowl of water, and began to chant. All of a sudden, the water turned a greenish hue and the water started to bubble and swirl. Just then the water went calm and still once again.

Suddenly a distorted image appeared in the water, seconds later the image began getting more and more clear. It was a male figure with pointy ears and long silky black hair. He had a short goatee and had a muscular thick face.

"I am sorry to disturb you but I would like to speak to one of the Elemental Centaurs. We would like to implore their help," Ruth said.

"I am he who you are looking for. I am Metatronas. One of the last two remaining Elemental Centaurs," the creature said.

"What happened to the other Elemental Centaurs," Ruth asked.

"We were hunted down and killed off by a great evil," Metatronas replied to the question in a deep strong voice. "Now, what help do you need?"

"We implore your help to do battle against a great evil," Ruth explained.

"We Elemental Centaurs will discuss the matter and let you know," Metatronas said to them. "Do you intend for the children to battle as well?" he asked motioning to Isaiah, Madison, and Brandon.

"Yes, they are the ones who will be battling," Ruth replied.

"Take this to heart. If they go into battle, it will come at a great cost," Metatronas said.

"What do you mean?" Ruth asked.

"If they do battle, they will lose a piece of themselves," Metatronas answered.

All of a sudden, Metatronas' image slowly faded. There was a long silence; and Ruth, Lenn, and the kids waited patiently for him. Moments later the water began swirling once again and Metatronas' image reappeared in it.

"I have spoken with my fellow Elemental Centaur and we both agreed that we will help you in the battle," Metatronas said to Ruth. "You will have to open a Temporal-Lobe of Anubus. It can only be opened at a full moon."

"The next full moon will be morrow. I will make the preparations," Ruth said to Metatronas.

Right then Metatrons' image faded away and the water became calm again. Ruth threw out the water from the bowl. Lenn left the farm and everyone went to sleep. The following morning Ruth and the kids woke up early and got ready for the day. After finishing the morning chores and eating breakfast, they began battle training. When training was over, they washed up in the stream and had some lunch. When they were finished eating, Ruth washed the dishes and the children put them away.

Ruth hitched the wagon to the horses and they went to town. They looked around town slowly making their way to Lenn's shop. Nobody was there so they waited for Lenn, minutes later Lenn came back inside and smiled at them.

"How are you doing?" Lenn asked.

"We are good. You wanted to see us?" Isaiah asked.

"Well, I made two more pistols. And I have made new mini cannonball projectiles," Lenn replied.

Lenn led them to the workbench and pulled off the sheet.

"These are all three of the pistols. I have fashioned a holder so you can carry them with ease," Lenn told the kids. "These new mini cannonball projectiles are special. I made them sharp and pointed like a mace."

"But why would you change the mini cannonballs?" Madison asked.

"Because by fashioning them to be sharp and pointed like a mace it will be more effective against the Black Shadow," Lenn began to explain to them. "I also dipped the balls into holy water."

"Thank you so much for helping us," Ruth said smiling at Lenn.

"You are very welcome. Anytime," Lenn answered smiling back.

"Are you coming to the farm tonight to help us?" Ruth asked.

"Yes, I will be coming," Lenn replied.

Ruth kissed Lenn on the cheeks and she and the kids left the shop. When they got back to the farm, they began preparing to open the Temporal-Lobe of Anubus. Ruth grabbed the books she needed, and the children gathered the herbs, salts and other things. It slowly got darker and darker until the full moon rose high above Old York New shining brightly. A while later Lenn had returned and tied up his horse. He took out the pistols and the new mini cannonballs from a travel sack and handed them to the kids. The children went inside, put the objects away, and returned to Ruth and Lenn.

Ruth took the salts and began making a magical protective circle. She placed some magical herbs into a small bowl and smashed them up into a paste. Ruth spread the macerated herbs around the protective circle and softly chanted. She placed candles around the protective circle and lit them. Just then Lenn and the children entered the circle. Lenn and the kids circled around Ruth and held hands. Ruth opened another book to the middle and started chanting loudly. The flames of the candles began to dance around and all of a sudden, the flames shot up high into the air. An invisible energy field surrounded the protective circle and electricity shot through the air.

Suddenly a heavy gust of wind blew through the air and the magical portal, the Temporal-Lobe of Anubus opened. The portal slowly grew bigger and bigger until it was five yards high and five yards wide. Just then Metatronas and the other Elemental Centaur trotted out of the portal. Now that they could see Metatronas, they saw that he was all white. The other centaur had the upper body of a black woman and the lower torso of a tan Cheshire horse. Both centaurs had wooden staffs in their hands with ancient ruins carved into them.

Slowly Ruth stopped chanting and Lenn and the kids stopped holding hands. The energy field slowly faded away and the portal disappeared. The two centaurs slowly trotted over to Ruth, Lenn, and the kids and shook their hands.

"Thank you so much for agreeing to help us," Ruth said to Metatronas.

"It is our right and duty to fight for good and to help all beings in any and all realms," Metatronas answered Ruth. "This is Lightrina; we both form the last two of the Elemental Centaurs."

Lightrina smiled at them and shook their hands as well.

"She cannot speak. She lost the ability to speak in a battle ages ago," Metatronas said to them. "What is the dark evil you are fighting?"

"Would you mind if we explain to you morrow? I think we all need a good night's sleep," Ruth answered Metatronas. "Would you like any supper before you retire for the night?"

"No, we are fine, thank you. We will be retiring out here," Metatronas answered in his deep strong voice. "Goodnight to you all."

"Goodnight to the both of you as well," they replied.

Lenn left the farm and Ruth and the children went inside.

The following morning, they all woke up at the crack of dawn and got ready. Metatronas and Lightrina helped with the chores. After, they sat outside at the workbench and had a breakfast of porridge and roasted mushrooms. A while later Lenn came over to the farm and they all started talking.

"I promised to tell you why we implored you for help," Ruth began to say. "We are battling a great evil called the Black Shadows."

"They have taken control of the mind of Keals, the heir in the line of succession to the throne," Lenn quickly added. "They have also done something to our true king, Lord Devon."

"We know of this evil known as the Black Shadows. They are the demons that hunted and killed off us Elemental Centaurs," Metatronas said balling up his hands into fists. "We will help you in this battle. And we shall defeat them."

"First we must find and retrieve the holy weapon known as the Eye of God," Isaiah said.

"Oh yes, we Elemental Centaurs know of the Eye of God as well," Metatronas said to them.

"My Great Grandfather Chacko Mathais led the group that hid the Eye of God," Isaiah told Metatronas and Lightrina. "We are reforming that group."

"It is good to know that the descendant of Chacko Mathais is putting the Warriors of Raw back together again," Metatronas said.

"How do you know about the Warriors of Raw?" Isaiah asked.

"All the Elemental Centaurs know of the Eye of God and the Warriors of Raw," Metatronas started explaining. "Actually, the first order of the Elemental Centaurs made the Eye of God."

"Tell us about it," Isaiah said in curiosity.

"That is a story I will tell you at another time," Metatronas answered, and he turned to Ruth and Lenn. "We will start our journey to find the Eye of God morrow."

They began battle training and Metatronas and Lightrina joined them. Later that evening the children showed Metatronas and Lightrina the pistols and mini cannonballs.

Chapter 14

Journey to Find the Eye of God

The following morning, they started making preparations for their journey. They began putting sacks filled with provisions of bread, mushrooms, and canteens filled with water onto the wagon. A little while later, Lenn arrived at the farm and unloaded some more provisions onto the wagon. Then he took out a wooden box and opened it to reveal three dozen mini cannonballs.

"These are the mini cannonballs you told me to make for the mission. I could not make any more without people asking questions," Lenn said.

"Let us go get ready. We must leave right away," Metatronas said.

The children put on their armor, strapped on the holder for their weapons, and put their weapons in them. Then Ruth and Lenn hitched the wagon to two horses and they hopped on the wagon. Moments later the kids got on the wagon and they all left. A while later they reached the edge of the main village of Old York New. Isaiah took out Mathais' map and they looked at it. Moments later he put it away and they kept on moving. It slowly got darker and darker so they stopped and made camp.

The next day they all woke up very early, packed up, and continued on their journey. They slowly entered a heavily wooded area. A couple of hours later they had finally come to the border of Old York New and a neighboring kingdom. The rode was split in three ways so they took the middle path. They walked in silence for minutes through the sweet-smelling forest, the dried Oak leaves gentle under their feet, and above them wind made a beautiful song in the branches. A large black rat scuttled a few feet in front of them and disappeared under a bush. The shadows of the trees were long and twisted and there was a heavy, sweet, spring aroma to the air. The children stumbled on large heavy roots and the adults helped them up off the ground.

Hours later it got darker until the moon was high above the land. They set up camp and slept for the night.

The following morning, they had breakfast, packed everything up, and began their journey once again. Meanwhile at the castle, the Black Shadows were in the throne room talking to each other. Just then Keals walked into the room.

"There is a small group that is going after a weapon to stop us," Keals announced in fear.

"Don't worry, we have ways to stop them," Supay said smirking.

The eyes of the Black Shadow started glowing. The floor of the throne room quacked heavily and it opened up. Slowly hellhound dogs rose out of the ground. The hellhounds' eyes began to glow brightly. Their skin was translucent and peeling away, and their pumping blood vessels were visible. There were long razor-sharp jagged spikes protruding out of their backs. The Black Shadow's eyes started glowing and in return the hellhounds' eyes began glowing. All of a sudden, the group of hellhounds sunk back down into the ground.

Meanwhile, the small group of travelers were on a narrow pathway. There were loud sounds of leaves crunching and twigs snapping. Four small mounds appeared in the ground and moved towards them. Suddenly, the hellhounds rose out of the ground with glowing eyes, and Lightrina pointed towards the hellhounds. Just then, the hellhounds began attacking them. Lightrina slammed her staff on the ground and an energy force shot out of the wooden staff. It hit one of the hellhounds; it flew into the air and hit a tree with a loud thud. The kids took their swords, shoved them into two hellhounds, and pulled them out. Their wounds started bubbling and sizzling and the creatures wailed in agony. The hellhounds' eyes rolled back; started glowing and they began attacking them again.

Lightrina made a symbol in the air with her fingers and clapped her hands twice, the sign in the air started to flame up. Two fireballs shot out of the flaming sign hitting two hellhounds. The evil creatures whimpered in agony and turned into ashes. One of the hellhounds jumped onto Lightrina's hind legs, the hound's jaws unhinged like a snake and bit down. Its jaws clamped down and locked in. Madison shoved her sword once again into the hellhound. It whimpered in pain and let go. Lightrina and Metatronas started slamming their staffs into the bodies of the hellhounds, and the hounds fell to the ground motionless.

All of a sudden, Lightrina's legs buckled underneath herself and she fell to the ground. Metatronas placed his hands over Lightrina's wounds the hellhound inflicted and closed his eyes. The wounds sizzled and burned, and slowly closed up. Ruth smashed herbs into a paste and rubbed the paste on the area.

"Are you okay?" Brandon asked.

Lightrina shook her head up and down and started signing with her fingers.

"She says she is okay, but I do not think she is being truthful," Metatronas said to them. "We should stay here for the night so she can heal."

They set up camp and the kids started a fire. After eating lunch Metatronas and Lightrina took the children aside and started teaching them sign language. It slowly got darker and darker until a crescent moon was high above the land. Everybody was sleeping except for Metatronas and Isaiah; they sat staring into the crackling fire.

"Remember I told you that I would tell you how the Eye of God came to exist. Well, this is how it happened," Metatronas said.

Just then he began telling the tale.

It was sometime after Lucifer was cast out of Heaven and into Hell. God knew that Lucifer and his demons would wage war against him and his heavenly forces. So, God called upon a group of centaurs and gave four centaurs each the powers of the four elements. God chose one particular centaur to wield the powers of all four elements, and he was to lead the Elemental Centaurs.

God then gathered all the Elemental Centaurs and instructed them to make a weapon for mortal beings to fight against Lucifer and his demons. So, the original Elemental Centaurs forged the Eye of God. And from then on, the Eye of God has been passed down to the ones of the purest of worth to wield it and fight great evil.

"But how would we find out if we are worthy?" Isaiah asked.

"If you are worthy, a sign will be shown to you," Metatronas answered him back. "Now young Isaiah, why have you decided to put the Warriors of Raw back together?"

Then Isaiah started explaining everything to Metatronas.

"This is a very noble deed for you children. You will be blessed," Metatronas said making the sign of the cross on top of Isaiah's forehead. As he did this, a cross shined on Brandon and Madison's foreheads. "You go and rest. I will take up first watch."

Isaiah continued to stare into the flames until he fell asleep.

Early the following morning they all got up before the crack of dawn. Ruth and Metatronas asked Lightrina how she was feeling; she began walking around to show them she was better. After breakfast, Isaiah looked at the map once again. After they packed up their stuff and left. They all kept ever vigilant for demons and other enemies. The forest slowly faded to an end, and a lush beautiful large meadow began and ran for miles. As they continued on their journey, the centaurs taught their new companions some more sign language. Slowly the lush green meadow faded away and the rocks of a mountainous gorge terrain began.

They slowly entered a dangerous desolate place called the Valley of the Lost. The land began to form these bulky protrusions that looked like large granite-like sandy mounds. They had a definite, recurring form, but they were not precipices. It was as if they were on the back of some sandy beings. After a while of traveling in the Valley of the Lost, the strange and uneasy feeling and atmosphere of the Valley of the Lost took its toll on the travelers. As they were walking they slowly began sinking, it was quicksand. Metatronas and Lightrina quickly pushed the wagon and horses out into safety. They sank deeper and deeper into the quicksand and suddenly stopped. Lightrina and Metatronas took their staffs and rose them high into the air. The centaurs' eyes began to glow brightly and their staffs lit up with flames, and they slammed their staffs into the quicksand.

All of a sudden, the quicksand was engulfed by flames, but not harming the travelers. The bed of quicksand quickly dried up turning it into cement. Metatronas and Lightrina started slamming their fists into the newly formed cement. The cement cracked and crumbled underneath their fists. The centaurs jumped free and hoisted their companions to safety.

"We will be back. We must stretch out our wings," Metatronas said.

He and Lightrina shot into the sky with their magnificent wings outstretched, flapped them a few times, and came back to the ground gently again. Metatronas looked at the map and put it away, informing them that it would be safer for him and Lightrina to lead them. As they walked, the centaurs took their staffs and hit the ground to see if there were any more quicksand beds. The chirping and buzzing of insects made it more difficult to concentrate on their work.

The sun's sweltering rays beat down on them, making it feel even hotter than it was. The kids took off their armor to make it feel more bearable but kept their weapons at the ready just in case. Hours later, it slowly got darker and darker and the evening air got cooler in the Valley of the Lost. They set up camp and after having dinner, they went to sleep.

During the night, the atmosphere became foggy and Isaiah tossed and turned from not being able to sleep. All of a sudden, the earth quaked and a large crack ripped through the ground. Just then, Isaiah began falling into the hole and kept falling into what felt like a deep, dark, endless gorge. He landed hard on hard sandy ground. Isaiah slowly got up and tried to see through the darkness but couldn't. Just then fire surrounded him rising high above his head. The sand swirled around slow at first and then faster and faster, seconds later the sand dissolved from underneath his feet. Lying there in front of him was an ancient-looking torch; it was the Eye of God. Suddenly Isaiah quickly woke up and everything came into focus. It was a dream, but it felt so very real.

Isaiah looked up at the crackling fire and saw Metatronas looking at him. He sat up and told the centaur about the dream. Metatronas listened intently to Isaiah and then told him to go back to sleep. Early the next morning Brandon and Madison told Isaiah about a dream they both had, it was the same dream. A little while later they started packing up the camp.

"What do you think that was?" the kids asked the centaurs.

"It sounds like it was the vision of the Eye of God," Metatronas said answering the kids. "Now go put on your armor. We will be leaving shortly."

"How long of traveling do we have left?" Lenn asked.

"We have until noon to reach the end of the Valley of the Lost. Then we should reach the desert of Tyme," Metatronas quickly answered. "That is where the Eye of God is hidden."

They slowly left their present location and finished their last leg in the Valley of the Lost. By late afternoon they entered the very hot and dry desert of Tyme. The sun's rays beat down stronger and more fierce on the travelers making it hotter than it was in the Valley of the Lost. As they traveled deeper and deeper into the desert of Tyme it got hotter and hotter. Suddenly from a distance, the children saw a lumpy mound moving towards them in the sand. Seconds later, something jumped out of the sand; it was a demon.

The demon was made up entirely of sand, it looked similar to the hellhounds but it stood up like human beings. Metatronas told them that the demon was a desert sand demon. Slowly, one by one, a group of sand demons rose out of the sand until the travelers were surrounded. The demons started snarling and howling, and attacked them. The centaurs slammed their staffs into the sand; the demons got thrust high into the air and hit the sand again with a loud thud.

One of the demons' sandy arms began distorting and dissolving and the demon shot sand out at the kids, they fell back landing hard on the ground. Ruth started chanting and a demon began wailing in agony and it combusted into flames. At that moment another sand demon snarled hungrily and slashed deeply into the hind legs of Lightrina. The children saw what happened and thrust their swords into the sand demon, it wailed and screamed in pain as the wound burned and sizzled. The demon pulled its claw out of Lightrina's hind legs and combusted into flames.

The children loaded the pistols and shot at three demons, the mini cannonballs made a cracking sound as they sped through the air hitting the demons. Nothing happened for a minute, and then the demons burned and turned into ashes. Just then the remainder of the surviving demons jumped back into the sand and swam away like sea creatures. Lightrina's hind legs buckled from underneath her and she fell, blood oozed out of the wound. Metatronas touched Lightrina with his healing hands and the wound slowly closed up.

"Will she be all right?" Madison asked.

"I think so, but I do not think she will be able to fight in the battle against the Black Shadow," Metatronas answered.

"I think you should stay off your legs for a while," Ruth said to Lightrina as she signed as well. "I am so sorry for doing this to you."

Ruth stood up and whispered into Metatronas' ears,

"That is a good idea." Metatronas answered.

Metatronas slowly began lifting up Lightrina with Ruth's and Lenn's help to place her on the wagon. Isaiah unhitched the wagon and Metatronas lifted it and they continued on their journey. The fury of the sun beat down on them unbearably. With the extra weight on Metatronas, it strained his back making their traveling even slower. It slowly got darker so they stopped and set up camp. Even though it was still hot, the night air was less sweltering than the day. Demons started surrounding their campsite, so Ruth placed a protection spell around the campsite. Then each of them took turns keeping watch.

The following morning, they all got up early, packed up their stuff, and quickly left before any demons would arrive again. As the morning progressed, it got even hotter as the sun's rays bared heavily on them. Morning slowly turned into noon as they reached the last leg of their journey in the desert of Tyme. An hour later they had reached the hiding place of the Eye of God, the Cave of Quartz.

Ruth took out two pieces of parchments and handed it to Madison. She informed them that there were protective incantations on the first parchment; the second parchment had a revealing incantation for the Eye of God. The children walked towards the entrance of the cave and quickly stopped; Ruth, Lenn, and Metatronas stood there steadfast. The children asked the adults why they weren't coming; they answered that they had to do this on their own. So, with their weapons securely at hand, they went into the cave.

The air was cooler in the cave than it was out in the desert. They walked through a very narrow passageway until they reached a cavern. All of a sudden, two desert demons and a group of Black Shadow followers rose out of the ground. The kids took their swords and shields and began to fight. Madison took out one of the folded pieces of parchments and began chanting. The demons and followers froze in suspended animation. The kids got to the end of the cavern and went through another narrow passageway. Moments later they entered a massive opened cavern. The kids, with their weapons still at the ready looked for the Eye of God. At that moment Madison remembered the piece of parchment and started saying the incantation.

Suddenly the right-hand corner of the cavern lit up brightly, so they went to that spot. They took out their spades and got ready to dig but did not need to. As it happened in their dreams, the sandy floor lit up with a ring of flames around the spot. The sand dissolved from that spot and a hole revealed itself. Inside the hole was a large cloth-wrapped bundle. Isaiah picked up and held the bundle tightly in his arms like it was a baby. As they left the cavern and passageway, they found the demons and the Black Shadows' followers were still frozen in suspended animation. Moments later the children slowly climbed out of the cave into the hot desert air, slowly their eyes adjusted to the bright sun. The kids walked down to where the adults were waiting. Isaiah put the bundle in the wagon where Lightrina was resting.

Metatronas and Lightrina smiled at the children. They quickly left the cave of Quartz and slowly made their way out of the desert of Tyme. Demons followed them and surrounded their campsite, but they didn't harm them because of the protection spell Ruth had placed around them. All night long the people who kept watch heard demonic howling, growling, and snarling. When daybreak had finally come, Madison was the first to wake up so she woke the others. They found that there were no more demons surrounding the campsite, so they quickly packed everything up and left.

Making excellent time, they exited the desert of Tyme and reached the end of the Valley of the Lost. By the end of the day, they were halfway there. They set up their last campsite and made some dinner. After eating, they went to sleep while Metatronas and Isaiah stayed up once again talking.

"When we get back to the farm, I will be returning to my world with Lightrina. But do not worry, I will be back to fight the Black Shadow with you," Metatronas whispered to Isaiah. "Both Lightrina and I have kept a secret from all of you."

"What secret are you keeping?" Isaiah asked with curiosity and worry.

"Lightrina is with child, she will bear my child. And the baby she is having will be the next Elemental Centaur," Metatronas whispered.

"That is great, but why would you keep that a secret?" Isaiah asked.

"Because she did not want you to worry about her and try to stop her from doing battle," Metatronas answered. "To tell you the truth I really did not want to come and fight at first because I was scared for her safety, but Lightrina convinced me."

They stayed up for a little while longer and talked until Ruth and Lenn took second watch.

The following morning they all woke up at the crack of dawn and packed up their stuff. Ruth asked Lightrina if she was feeling okay and she replied yes. By early evening they got back to the farm and prepared everything to open a Temporal-Lobe of Anubus. Just then the children signed with their hands to Lightrina. Isaiah promised Lightrina that they would bring Metatronas back to her. Ruth made the protective circle and Lenn and the children held hands all around her. The portal opened and Metatronas and Lightrina slowly walked through it.

A while later Metatronas came out of the portal again stained with blood. The portal quickly closed and Lenn and Ruth ran to him and asked what had happened, he replied that Lightrina is okay but he had to fight off three centaurs that were possessed by demons. Metatronas washed up in the stream and Isaiah and his uncle Lenn started talking.

"I think I have a better way for the mini cannonballs to work better against the demons," Isaiah said.

"How can I make it better," Lenn asked.

"Well, keep the mini cannonballs sharp and mace like. Just make them hollowed out; if the inside is hollow, you can fill them with holy water," Isaiah started explaining to Lenn. "This way when the mini cannonballs hit the demons, they will explode with holy water affecting them even faster."

"That is a great idea," Lenn commented.

Moments later the others joined in the conversation and the rest of the evening went by quietly.

Chapter 15
The Final Battle

The heat of the summer finally arrived in Old York New. Shop and stand owners were afraid to come to town because of the actions of the Black Shadow. The Black Shadow did as he pleased and feasted on anything. It didn't try to hide its dark wickedness at all. It would unhinge its jaws and devour people whenever it wanted. Keals didn't even try to hide or stop the Black Shadow.

At about that time Metatronas was filling a bowl with water and herbs when Ruth started chanting.

The water started swirling around and turned a grayish hue and like before Lightrina's image appeared in the water. Metatronas smiled at Lightrina and they began talking. A while had passed and Lightrina's image faded away and Ruth threw out the water from the bowl. They began doing the afternoon chores and Metatronas helped them.

Later Metatronas took Isaiah aside and talked with him. Throughout the course of the day, the air got unbearably hot so they cooled off in the stream and went under the shade of a tree and rested. Metatronas took Isaiah aside once again.

"I think it is time to open the bundle," Metatronas said.

"Are you sure?" Isaiah asked.

"Yes, I am," Metatronas answered.

Isaiah went inside to his room, grabbed the cloth wrapped bundle, and went back outside to the others. He unwound the cloth wrapping slowly revealing the Eye of God. Although it was ancient, it wasn't rusted like it should have been. Also in the bundle was a wrinkled rolled up piece of parchment. He took it and unrolled it, there were words written on it. Isaiah asked what was written on the parchment and Metatronas told him it is the words to say to cast the demons back to hell when the torch is lit.

All of a sudden, a messenger hawk swooped above their heads and slowly landed on Isaiah's shoulder.

Meanwhile back at the castle, the Black Shadow was in the catacombs surrounding a pool of blood. It started chanting and the blood started bubbling, Lilith slowly appeared.

"So, what's happening with our plans?" Lilith asked.

"The next blood moon is in three days' time. And all the preparations have been made," Supay said with an evil smile on his face. "And all the followers know what to do, and we also have the sacrifices we need."

"That's good, I'll soon be free of this prison and I'll have my revenge on all the filthy fleshlings," Lilith said.

The sun slowly set getting darker and darker as the moon rose high above Old York New. Back at the farm, they were just finishing up the evening chores when they saw a wagon approaching, it was Lenn. The wagon slowly came to a halt at the back of the cabin, and Lenn hopped off. He shook Metatronas' hand and hugged the others. Then he motioned for them to come over to the wagon, so they went.

"Is this why you sent us word that you were coming?" Isaiah asked.

"Yes, it is," Lenn answered.

Then he pulled the sheet off the wagon to reveal a medium-sized box and six crossbows. The crossbows had a slightly different look to them. Then he opened up the box, inside were dozens of new mini cannonballs.

"So, with the mini cannonball projectiles, I did what Isaiah suggested. I hollowed them out and fill them with holy water," Lenn started to explain. "Now when they hit their targets, they explode and holy water will gush out."

"What is so special about these crossbows?" Brandon asked.

"Well, you could load four arrows at a time and shoot them at once," Lenn quickly answered. "Bring out your pistols."

The children quickly ran into the cabin, grabbed the pistols, and came back outside. Lenn tied a stuffed sack to a tree, and the children loaded the pistols and shot them. They hit the sack the projectiles exploded and holy water gushed out. Moments later, he unloaded the crossbows and the boxes from the wagon, and showed them how they worked. At twilight, everyone bid each other farewell.

The following day Ruth, Brandon, and Madison came over. Metatronas and the children began battle training while Ruth took her books and did research. A little while later Ruth tied a rolled-up piece of parchment and sent it out with a messenger hawk. Then went back inside and did some more research.

Sometime later Ruth came back out and joined the others in training. Later that afternoon Lenn had come over and greeted them. Then they went to the workbench in the back and started talking.

"I have done some more research and I think the Black Shadows are planning something big," Ruth said.

"But what exactly are they planning?" Lenn asked.

"I am not such but my books indicate that they are going to bring forth something. I think a powerful demon or more than one," Ruth answered.

"When will this happen?" Isaiah asked.

"I am not sure. My books indicate that on that day there will be an eclipse in the day and that night there will be a blood moon," Ruth said.

"I may have some insight on that. If my senses are correct, these events shall occur morrow," Metatronas said.

"How do you know this?" Brandon asked.

"We Elemental Centaurs not only have the powers of the elements but we can foresee cosmic occurrences," Metatronas replied.

"It is time for lunch. I will go make us something to eat," Ruth said.

A while later Ruth came back outside with a steaming pot and bowls. She set the bowls on the workbench and ladled mushroom stew into them. Just then they all said grace and started eating. After doing the evening chores and eating dinner the children went to sleep, and the adults started talking.

"Tonight, I will be making protection amulets for us. As I told the children, this battle will be more dangerous than the rebellion. This would be the time to get out of this," Ruth said.

"Like I told you from the beginning, we are ready for whatever is going to happen to us," Lenn said.

Then Ruth turned to Metatronas "Did you say your final goodbyes to Lightrina just in case?"

"Yes, I have. And I have given her and our offspring my blessings," he replied.

They talked for a while longer and slowly Lenn left the farm. Just then Ruth started gathering all the stuff to make the protection amulets, and Metatronas helped to make them.

The following morning, they woke up at the crack of dawn and everyone got ready for the day. A little while later Lenn rode up on his wagon and a smaller cart was attached to it. In the wagon was an ample supply of arrows and the redesigned mini cannonballs, in the smaller cart was a pile of scrap metal and iron. Lenn unloaded the cart next to the workbench, and slowly began melting the scrap metal and iron together. When it was cool enough to work with, he and the kids fashioned the molten mixture into a chain net. When they were done, they dipped it in holy water and named it the Snaggle Anchor.

Suddenly lightning and thunder ripped through the sky. Slowly inch by inch the moon moved closer and closer to the sun causing the eclipse. The lightning and thunder continued to rip through the sky. Ten minutes later, as fast as it had come the dark eclipse morning sky had cleared. Ruth told the kids to put their battle armor on and prepare for battle.

Meanwhile at the castle, one of the guards made his way to the prison. He grabbed one of the prisoners of the rebellion, locked the cells again, and dragged him to the catacombs and shackled him up between two pillars. Just then from out of the shadows came a group of hooded Black Shadows' followers. They circled around him holding hands and began chanting. Moments later the hooded followers' eyes rolled backward and the prisoner went into a hypnotic trance, and the followers chanted even louder.

Back at the farm, they were almost done getting ready. Ruth handed everybody one of the protection amulets and placed one on herself, then she chanted a protection incantation. They got on the horses with their weapons in hand and they all galloped away with Metatronas at the lead. All afternoon lightning and thunder ripped through the sky. Slowly the afternoon sky turned darker and darker until the moon was high above Old York New. The moon appeared to look red; it was the blood moon...

At the castle, the demons' followers were still chanting and the prisoner was still shackled up between the pillars in a hypnotic trance. At that moment Keals and a larger group of demon followers entered the catacombs and surrounded a large rectangular altar. All of a sudden, the planets slowly began to align perfectly and the ground shook. Two guards unshackled the hypnotized prisoner from the pillars and tied him up onto the stone altar. Keals and all the demon worshipers chanted ever louder. Slowly from out of the shadows came Supay. Three of the followers went to the stone altar and stood around it to form a triangle.

A moment later another follower cut off his own hand screaming in unimaginable agony. As the blood spilled out it formed a pool, slowly the pool of blood started to bubble. Just then Lilith appeared in the pool.

"Are we all ready?" Lilith asked.

"Yes, we're all prepared. We're about to perform the ritual," Supay answered.

The chanting got louder and louder, almost deafening. The Black Shadow went over to its followers that formed the triangle and slit their throats. Their lifeless bodies fell to the ground and their oozing blood formed a triangle outline. Supay went over to the stone altar and stabbed the tied-up prisoner in the chest and slit his throat as well. The blood acted like it had a life of its own moving all around the triangle. Keals and the other followers went into a hypnotic state and began chanting once again. Just then Supay walked to the three corners of the blood-filled triangle. The demon's eyes started glowing and they chanted, a crack ripped through the middle of the catacombs. Lilith pressed her long bony fingers against the barrier of the hellish prison. The barrier began to distort and slowly her finger went through it and Lilith smirked.

Meanwhile the kids, along with Lenn, Metatronas, and Ruth, were slowly making their way to the castle. A while later they got there and stuck to the shadows. All of a sudden, a small group of guards spotted them and attacked them. Moments later the guards were on the ground lifeless except for one.

"Where is the Black Shadow and his followers?" Ruth asked the guard as she twisted his arm and punched him in the nose.

"I will never tell you," the guard replied spitting at her.

"That was not very nice or smart," Ruth said while knocking him to the ground and extending his arm out. "Break it."

Metatronas reared up on his hind legs and came back down hard on the guard's arm. The guard's arm made a crunching sound and he screamed and cried in agony.

"Now, I can heal you but only if you tell us where they are," Ruth said.

"They are in the royal catacombs. Now please heal me," the guard begged.

"I would, but I do not want to," Ruth answered him and she turned to the others. "You all know what to do right?

"Yes, we do," they replied.

They slowly made their way to the catacombs keeping ever vigilant. All of a sudden, it appeared as though actual blood was oozing through the blood moon. Back in the catacombs, the Black Shadow and his followers were in the midst of doing the ritual to bring forth the demon queen. Thunder and lightning ripped through the sky, and the blood in the triangle started bubbling and twirling. Just then the Warriors of Raw entered the catacombs shooting arrows in every direction, hitting the chanting followers. Keals stepped aside and started chanting; all of a sudden, a group of the gargoyle creatures rose out of the ground and started attacking them.

Brandon quickly loaded his pistol and shot it. The projectiles hit two gargoyles in the chest exploding and holy water gushed out. They screamed as their wounds sizzled, and they turned into stone and ashes and dissolved. Lenn and Ruth shot their arrows into the large group of followers. Metatronas folded his hands together and slammed his fists into the dirt; thorns, vines, and roots shot up out of the ground and acting like hands took hold of two gargoyles. They clawed and gnawed, struggling to get free but to no avail. The roots and vines pulled even harder tearing them in half. Again, Metatronas slammed his fists into the ground, the ground opened under some Black Shadows' followers swallowing them up. Ruth started casting spell after spell in all directions.

The kids ran into the crowd of followers and began fighting them. Metatronas spun his staff in the air slamming it into the ground. A gust of wind shot out hitting Keals and the others, knocking them to the ground. He made a sign in the air and it began glowing. Balling his hands, he slammed his fists together. Water shot out of the sign hitting the last of the gargoyle creatures, they fell to the ground and turned into ashes. Once again, the ground shook really hard. Isaiah saw Supay and ran towards him; jumping on him. Isaiah punched him in the face and shoved a holy water dipped arrow into Supay's stomach, the wound burned and sizzled, and Supay pulled the arrow out.

Just then, Isaiah lit the Eye of God and repeated the activating words. The flames jumped, crackled, and shot high into the air, the fire twisted and went into Supay's mouth. Supay's demonic spirit came out struggling to get away and somehow broke free. All of a sudden, two bloody fingers slowly rose out of the blood-filled triangle.

"Look over there," Lenn said pointing to the triangle.

The kids, Ruth, and Metatronas turned around and saw what was happening.

"How are we going to stop that?" Madison asked.

"I do not know if we can," Ruth answered.

Slowly a bloody arm rose out of the blood-filled triangle. Supay's eyes shot open. He stared at the kids and snarled at them angrily.

"Who are you?" Supay asked.

"We are the Warriors of Raw," Isaiah replied.

"You filthy fleshlings can't stop us," Supay hissed.

"We will see about that," Madison said.

Lilith continued to slowly rise up out of the bloody triangle. Just then Supay started a demonic chant, his body distorted and turned into the large demon creature being. They ran towards each other and began fighting. Isaiah and Madison shot arrows into the creature's chest. It smirked then pulling the arrows out of its chest and then he shoved one of the arrows into Isaiah's arm. Isaiah cried in agony and fell onto the ground. The creature picked up Brandon and Madison and threw them; they hit a tree and fell hard. Ruth started chanting and an energy ball flew out of her hands hitting the demon in the face. It snarled at Ruth picking her up by the throat and threw her into a tombstone.

Metatronas made another sign in the air and slammed his hands together again, water shot out of the sign hitting the massive demon in the chest. Slowly ice surrounded the demon choking him. Lilith's blood covered body was halfway out of the triangle. Just then Metatronas opened his wings and flew into the air; moments later he came crashing back down with his fist out. He slammed into the demon knocking him off his feet. The demon hit a large tree and fell onto a tombstone motionless.

Isaiah threw the Eye of God over to Brandon and he caught it. Brandon said the words and the torch's flames went into the demon's mouth once more and sucked out Supay's demon spirit. The huge monstrous demon being slowly changed back into the councilperson. A black-hole opened up in the ground sucking up the Black Shadow and closed up again. Most of the demon followers scattered in all directions. A hand full stayed knowing what was coming. The ground shook for a third time, with one last push Lilith was finally free from her hellish prison.

All of a sudden, the blood that covered Lilith dried forming a hard coating. It slowly cracked and the blood coating exploded flying everywhere. Lilith's long black hair was matted, and her skin was pale white with scorch marks. Her piercing black eyes lit up like a blazing bonfire, and her tongue darted in and out like a serpent. She saw what happened and screamed in anger.

"What happened to my Black Shadow soldier?" Lilith asked.

"We cast it back to the bowels of hell. And we will do the same with you as well," Ruth replied.

"That's what you think! You stupid filthy fleshlings will never defeat me!" Lilith said.

They ran towards each other. Lilith punched Ruth in the chest and she flew across the graveyard. She picked up Brandon and Isaiah by the throat and hurled them into the air. Lilith stared at Madison with her fire blazing eyes and Madison began gasping for air. Metatronas spun his wooden staff and flames erupted from it. He slammed the flaming staff in Lilith's stomach, she fell to the ground, and Madison was able to breathe once again. Metatronas flew into the air and soared back down as fast as lightning; all of a sudden, Lilith jumped into the air and caught Metatronas in midair. She punched him in both wings and threw him down; he hit the ground forming a crater. Lilith came back to the ground and started hitting Metatronas until he was bloodied and battered.

Ruth snuck up behind Lilith and began chanting, the spell hit Lilith and she went flying across the graveyard; hitting a tombstone. The grave imploded underneath her; causing a crater. Lilith slowly got up and her eyes began glowing with anger. She jumped into the air and glided back down on top of Ruth punching her in the face. Ruth quickly pushed her away.

"Would you like to say hello to some people. I think they'd like to say hello to you," Lilith said.

Lilith's body started twisting and distorting and she slowly turned into two people, Scottie and Ruth's deceased husband.

"Mother, we are in pain and we are lonely," Scottie said.

"Honey, my dear, only you can help us. Come, join us," Ruth's deceased husband said.

"You are not real!" Ruth said with tears streaming down her face.

Ruth pulled a dagger out of her bosoms and threw it at the two. They distorted and slowly changed into Lilith once again; she pulled the dagger out of her stomach throwing it onto the ground and grinned.

"You're smarter than I thought, sorceress. But it doesn't matter, witch," Lilith said.

Lilith's eyes rolled back and the dagger flew into Ruth's stomach. As she pulled the dagger out, she fell to the ground and blood slowly oozed out. Madison saw what had happened and shot a round of mini cannonballs at Lilith. The projectiles went through her back and exploded, gushing out holy water. Madison shot another round at her legs. Lilith wailed in agony and her legs buckled underneath her. She started a demonic chant and more gargoyle creatures rose out of the ground.

The children saw the gargoyle creatures rising and started battling them. As Madison fought, she slowly made her way to Ruth and helped her to her feet.

"Are you okay?" Madison asked.

"I am fine. Do not worry about me. We must put a stop to Lilith and send her back to Hell," Ruth said.

"How are we going to do that? This demoness is too powerful for us to defeat," Madison said.

"I know she is very powerful but we must defeat her," Ruth whispered to her breathlessly. "Use the Snaggle Anchor to help restrain her. And have faith."

Madison ran over to Brandon and Isaiah and whispered into their ears. Brandon took out the Snaggle Anchor spun it in the air and threw it. It soared through the air with perfect aim and wrapped around Lilith. Then the three of them ran and jumped on top of her. She struggled to get free but to no avail. The gargoyle creatures flew around trying to help Lilith by attacking them. One of the gargoyles grabbed Madison and threw her into a tombstone. A minute later she got back up and began fighting again. Moments later, the gargoyle creatures were destroyed in piles of ashes. Lilith was still struggling to get free when the kids went back to her.

"It is time for you to die," Isaiah said.

"You stupid filthy fleshlings can't stop me," Lilith said.

"Shut up, you bitch," Madison said as she kicked Lilith in the chest.

Madison took her sword and plunged it into Lilith's stomach, twisting it. Then Isaiah took the Eye of God and lit it, and repeated the words 'I CAST YOU BACK TO THE ABYSS OF HELL' three times. The flame of the torch shot up higher than before, above their heads, wrapping itself all around Lilith's body. She struggled even harder to get free. With one last cry of agony and fear from Lilith, the flames wrenched and twisted her. The black-hole slowly opened in the ground, it sucked the demoness through and closed up again. Lenn and the kids helped Ruth back to her feet again and along with Metatronas as they left the castle.

THE END?

Epilogue

The seasons had come and gone. Two years had slowly gone by. Cheats was now a fully grown adult cheetah. Keals still had his wicked ways even though he wasn't under the control of the Black Shadows. Lenn had been put to death for helping the Warriors of Raw. Isaiah, Brandon, and Madison still fought against Keals' evil and Ruth continued to help them.

One beautiful summer day the children and Cheats were on their way back to the farm from town. Suddenly, from out of nowhere, an unusual gust of wind blew around and electricity shot around two trees. Just then, a portal slowly opened and four people wearing strange clothes fell out of it.

"Quickly, scatter now—" Isaiah whispered to them.

Lynn Mathai grew up in Queens, New York. He grew up with many disabilities, and although he worked through some, he still has many of them. He enjoys writing stories for his nephews and niece. He is an avid reader and has always enjoyed fantasy, science fiction, and adventure books.

www.ingramcontent.com/pod-product-compliance
Lightning Source LLC
Chambersburg PA
CBHW061133200626
46817CB00016B/1372